THE LATCH MAN

DCI Blizzard investigates old rivalries that've resulted in murder

JOHN DEAN

Paperback published by The Book Folks

London, 2020

This book is a work of fiction. Names, characters, businesses, organizations, places and events are either the product of the author's imagination or are used fictitiously. Any resemblance to actual persons, living or dead, events or locales is entirely coincidental.

ISBN 979-8-6505-9945-6

www.thebookfolks.com

The Latch Man is the eighth standalone title in a series of British detective novels featuring Detective Chief Inspector John Blizzard. Look out for the other books in the series: The Long Dead, Strange Little Girl, The Railway Man, The Secrets Man, A Breach of Trust, Death List, and A Flicker in the Night.

Prologue

He arrived at the cottage in the village of Caitby Mallard shortly before one in the morning, walking softly down the side path and round to the back door. After standing and listening for a few moments, he tried the handle. It did not yield to his touch so the man reached into his jacket pocket and produced a screwdriver. Within a minute, he was stepping into the darkened cottage. He paused again to listen, then produced a torch by whose beam he picked his way across the kitchen and into the hallway.

After taking a few paces, he pushed open the door into the living room, struck by the clammy heat even though the summer sun had gone down several hours previously. He picked his way over to the dresser where he started searching through the top drawer. A sound behind him made him turn and shine his torch into the darkness to find himself staring into the wide-eyed face of an elderly woman.

Chapter one

'What we need,' said Detective Chief Inspector John Blizzard, looking up from the report he was reading as the sergeant walked into his office, 'is an interesting sort of murder.'

'And there was me thinking they were all interesting,' said David Colley. He sat down heavily opposite his boss. 'Boy, but it's scadding out there.'

'And if you were to translate that into English, it would mean what exactly?'

'It's a trifle warm in the vicinity of the police station precincts.'

'That's better,' said Blizzard.

It was afternoon and they were sitting in the chief inspector's stifling office at Abbey Road Police Station. The northern city of Hafton was in the middle of a heatwave – some said it would turn out to be the hottest August in thirty-five years – and the tar on the station car park was starting to melt, the paths were dust-dry and the light flared off the roofs of the houses on the main road. Even neglected houses that normally looked gloomy and unattractive, with their weed-infested driveways and crumbling pebbledash, assumed a strange kind of allure when caught in the rays of the blinding sun.

If the streets were hot, then Abbey Road Police Station was worse. Constructed as a temporary measure, the single-storey station was still there four decades later, the green paint on its prefabs peeling and the air conditioning system decrepit and ineffective. It had broken down yet again two days previously and those unfortunate enough to be in the station that afternoon were broiling as the sun beat mercilessly down on the flat roof. Blizzard himself presented a ragged sight. Perspiring freely, sweat glistening on his brow and dribbling down his face, shirt sleeves rolled up, dark patches under the arms, he was growing increasingly irritable as the temperature crept above ninety for the eighth day on the trot. Having spent a couple of hours sifting through reports, feeling his eyelids growing heavy, he welcomed the intervention from his sergeant.

'You know what I mean about murders.' The chief inspector gestured to the report that Colley had just dropped on the pile on his desk. 'I assume that's the one from over on the Larchgrove Estate?'

'It is.'

'Well, it proves my point,' said Blizzard. 'How long did it take you to solve it?'

'Ten minutes. A neighbour found him behind the lawnmower in his shed. We thought someone had grassed him up.'

Colley waited for the chief inspector to laugh at the joke but all Blizzard did was raise his eyes to the ceiling.

'Your humour gets worse,' he said. 'But the case makes my point beautifully. I mean, ten minutes, what kind of a challenge is that? And that one last week when the bloke walloped his mate with a snooker cue after they'd had fifteen pints each? How long did that take to solve?'

'Seven minutes and it only took that long because I stopped for a cup of tea.'

'Exactly my point,' said Blizzard. He walked over to the window and stared moodily out at the car park. 'It's not exactly Sherlock Holmes stuff, is it?'

'I thought we liked quick clear-ups because it keeps the chief constable happy.'

'We do but when was the last case where we really had to get the grey cells working?' Blizzard returned to the desk and took a swig out of his bottle of water. 'The trouble is that the Brits just do not know how to do summer. Every time we get a bit of sun…'

Colley grinned. He had heard the spiel plenty of times over recent days; any second now, Blizzard would make the lobster comment.

'…everyone strips down to their underpants, goes out into the garden, turns as red as a lobster…'

Not bad, thought Colley; two seconds this time. The reference to the chief inspector's beloved Italy could not be more than a few more seconds away.

'…drinks far too much, grabs the nearest weapon and knocks seven shades of shite out of the person standing closest. Now on the Continent – Italy, for example.'

'And do they never have any murders in Italy?' asked Colley innocently.

Blizzard studied the sergeant affectionately. Not many people could get away with such an intervention but David Colley was one of them. They were very different characters. Blizzard, broad-chested and slightly heavier than a man of five foot ten inches should be, had brown hair tousled as usual, eyes clear blue and chin showing the first signs of afternoon shadow. He was dressed in his customary dark suit with red tie dangling loosely at half-mast and pale blue shirt creased where he had been leaning back in his chair as he read the reports. Colley was different. A decade younger and tall and lean, today, as always, the sergeant's black hair was neatly combed, his round, most boyish, face showed no signs of stubble and his black trousers and dark blue shirt – buttoned to the top

– had all been perfectly ironed by Jay. His black shoes shone as usual. Despite the heat, he was hardly sweating.

'Sorry,' said Blizzard. He dabbed his face with a soggy handkerchief. 'But I'm hot and I'm bored.'

'In which case, I have a burglary that you might like to take a look at.'

'*You* do burglaries.'

'Yes, but it sounds like it could be our man again.'

'You talked to the victim?'

'Yes, but she refuses to talk to anyone but you, for some reason. Some old dear in Caitby Mallard.' Colley glanced down at his notebook. 'Hornsby. Doris Hornsby.'

'Doris Hornsby,' said Blizzard with a low whistle. He jumped to his feet, grabbed his jacket and headed for the door. 'This I've got to see. Come on.'

The startled sergeant watched in bemusement as the chief inspector almost sprinted into the corridor, colliding with a passing secretary and causing her to spill her cup of coffee. After mumbling an apology and dabbing half-heartedly at her with a handkerchief, Blizzard strode away at pace.

'Why so excited?' asked Colley as he caught his boss up near the door to the car park. 'Who on earth is Doris Hornsby? I've never heard of her.'

'Then you're in for a treat, young man,' said Blizzard as he pushed his way into the bright afternoon sunlight. 'Let's just say that this will be a bit of an education for you.'

Chapter two

'So who is she?' asked Colley for the third time. He was growing impatient at the chief inspector's knowing smiles as he refused to answer the question.

They were in Blizzard's car, heading for the picture-postcard village of Caitby Mallard several miles to the west of Hafton. It was a place that illustrated perfectly the contrasts within the sprawling Western Division. In the city could be found neglected Victorian terraces owned by landlords who had turned them into bedsits populated with drug addicts, alcoholics and drop-outs, and housing estates where weeds poked up between cracks in quadrangle floors littered with broken bottles, fast food cartons and syringes. However, to leave the city was to enter another world and now Blizzard was guiding the car through narrow hedge-lined country roads.

'Doris Hornsby,' said Blizzard, 'is a real celebrity. I did not even know that she was still alive. She must be well into her eighties. Possibly nineties.'

'Yes, but who is she?' asked the sergeant. Visions of an aristocratic blue-rinse old girl dripping in pearls popped into his mind. 'An artist, a writer, an actress, something glamorous like that?'

'It depends how you define glamorous. Actually, she's criminal royalty.'

'What, an old dear like that!' exclaimed the sergeant.

'The problem with young people today,' said Blizzard, as he slowed the car down at a crossroads, 'is that they forget that "old dears" were once young.'

'Point taken.' There was the merest hint of a smile in the sergeant's voice. 'Didn't mean to offend. Did you remember to pack your Zimmer frame? We may have to do some walking when we get there.'

'You can use it for the walk back to the station,' growled Blizzard.

They were now deep into the farming flatlands beyond the city. It was an area that the chief inspector knew well because Blizzard and his partner and baby son lived in a detached house on a new development in one of the villages not far from Caitby Mallard.

Colley looked over the fields as Blizzard piloted the car through the network of small hedge-lined lanes, half of which did not have road signs. For a detective who spent most of his time in the inner city, it was a pleasant change.

'Glad you know where you are going,' said the sergeant. 'So, what kind of criminal royalty is Doris then?'

'She was the matriarch of one of the greatest crime families the city has ever known. Possibly the greatest. And it must be something important for her to seek police help. She's never had anything to do with us before.'

'Still don't recognise the name, I am afraid.'

'How about George Leys?'

'Ah,' said Colley. 'No wonder you were so interested. Where does he fit into the picture?'

'First husband. She remarried after he was murdered.'

'Which was when?'

'Now you're asking,' said Blizzard as the car entered the village. 'Must be thirty, forty years ago. What's the address?'

'Lane End, left at the shop,' said Colley. He looked at the crooked little cottages huddled round a picturesque green complete with duck pond. 'This is nice. Not sure that I've ever been here. George Leys was shot, wasn't he?'

'Yeah, blasted with a shotgun as he left a boozer late one night. Part of a turf war. Some wide boy from London did it – his lot were trying to muscle in on George's protection racket.'

'And Doris carried on the family business after he died?'

'She'd have you believe that she didn't. From what I heard, after George's death, dear old Doris appeared to drop out of the crime business and surprised everyone by marrying a chap called Alf Hornsby instead. Funny little fellow, horn-rimmed spectacles, dapper suits, very quiet, exactly the opposite of George. Ran a pawnbrokers not far from the railway station. It wasn't much to look at but word was that he left Doris a small fortune when he died. Or at least that's what she told the taxman.'

'Hence her being able to live here,' said the sergeant as they pulled up outside a small stone ivy-covered cottage with a neatly-kept front garden full of roses. 'I seem to recall that there were two sons?'

'Yeah.' Blizzard cut the engine. 'Eric was his dad's right-hand man. Everyone expected him to take over the family firm after the murder but he got cold feet and fled the city. He was killed in a car crash in Spain. No great loss, really. Eric Leys was a nasty piece of work.'

'And the other son?'

'Martin was the straight one. An accountant. Changed his name to Hornsby to escape the stigma.' The detectives got out of the car and walked up to a sturdy oak front door complete with brass knocker. 'Retired now, I think.'

Blizzard rapped on the door, which was opened by a nurse, a plump woman in her fifties who gestured them into the cottage. The living room was dim – the curtains were drawn – and sweltering because the windows were closed and the gas fire was on despite the mid-afternoon temperature outside.

It took the officers a second or two to accustom their eyes to the gloom as they picked their way between the armchair and an occasional table to stand in front of the single bed on which lay Doris Hornsby, propped up on cushions. They gazed upon her emaciated features with morbid fascination. Her stick-like frame was encased in a pale blue nightie on top of which was a fluffy dressing gown, also pale blue. She wore carpet slippers, above which the detectives could see alabaster-white legs, veined and ribbed with age and sparrow-thin. Her hands, resting on her lap, also played testament to the passing of the years, the fingers gnarled and crabby, liver spots freckling the stretched paper-thin skin.

However, it was her face that drew the officers' gaze. Beneath the incongruous thick wavy ginger-tinged peppery hair – got to be dyed, mused Blizzard – were sunken cheekbones and thickly plastered make-up that could not conceal the lines that rivered her features. But if she was old, she was still sharp and surveyed the officers with clear blue eyes. A faint smile played on thin lips daubed with garish red lipstick, which jarred horribly with her pale features.

'Doris Hornsby as I live and breathe,' said the chief inspector. 'Or should I say Doris Leys?'

'I prefer Hornsby,' she said in a quavering voice.

'I'll bet you do.'

'And this young man is?' Doris flapped a hand in the sergeant's direction.

'Detective Sergeant David Colley.' Blizzard sat on the chair offered by the nurse and loosened his tie. 'So, what was so important to drag me out all this way, Doris?'

The inspector dabbed his brow with his handkerchief and glanced at the fire then at the nurse, who shrugged.

'I am sorry about the heat,' said Doris. 'But I have poor circulation. I cannot remember the last time I felt warm.'

Blizzard mopped his brow again, acutely conscious of how clammy his hands had become.

'So, what can we do for you?' he asked.

'I had a man in my bedroom last night.'

'Are you boasting or complaining?'

'Not a comment that does you justice, Chief Inspector.' She looked at him accusingly. 'I am sure Mr Gordon would not have made such an unkind comment.'

'Who?'

'One of your predecessors – the detective chief inspector who investigated poor George's death. Such a nice man.' She looked pointedly at Blizzard. 'Very polite.'

'Sorry, didn't know him.'

'He dressed smarter than you,' she said and surveyed the crumpled suit with distaste.

Blizzard ignored the comment.

'And how do you know the man was here?' he asked.

'I saw him. I take a sleeping pill at night – the nurse leaves it by bedside before she goes home – but I am never quite sure if I have taken it or not. I am afraid that I am getting rather forgetful these days. Anyway, I saw him searching through my drawers.' She nodded at the dresser.

'About what time?'

'I don't really know. Midnight, one – something like that. I have little sense of time at night.'

'Did you speak to him?' asked Blizzard.

'No, but when he saw me sitting up, he gave a little bow and disappeared into the hallway.'

'A little bow?'

'Yes.' She smiled. 'Rather gentlemanly, don't you think?'

'I don't think many criminals are gentlemen, Doris. Was anything taken?'

'We can find nothing missing,' said the nurse. 'One thing Mrs Hornsby has not mentioned is that he left the front door unlocked when he left.'

Blizzard exchanged a look with Colley.

'So, what did he look like, Doris?' asked the sergeant.

'It was difficult to see in the dark. Rather tall. I got the impression that he was a touch overweight, a bit like your chief inspector here.'

She winked at the sergeant, who tried to keep a straight face. Blizzard harrumphed but the sergeant noticed him pull his stomach in a little bit. The chief inspector had become sensitive about the extra pounds he was putting on after a recent newspaper picture of him at a press conference clearly showed his double chin.

'Did you recognise him?' asked Blizzard.

'I am afraid not.'

Blizzard thought he detected just the faintest hesitation.

'You don't seem sure,' he said.

'Oh, I am sure.'

'I hate to say this, but is there a possibility that you imagined it? Perhaps you dreamed it.'

'I definitely saw a man standing in my bedroom.' The look defied him to disagree.

'OK,' said Blizzard. He stood up; he was desperate to flee into the open air as his head had started to spin in the heat. 'I'll get forensics to come and check the place over.'

'I don't suppose there is the chance of a police officer to stay the night, is there? That is why I wanted to see you, Chief Inspector. I'm not really interested if you catch him nor not, I just want some protection.'

'I'll ask uniform to wheel round here from time to time.'

'I was hoping for a little more than that,' said Doris. 'Perhaps an officer on the door for a night or two?'

'It doesn't work like that,' said Blizzard.

'Mr Gordon–'

'Has long since retired.'

'Do you think it was The Latch Man?' asked the nurse, as Blizzard headed for the door.'

'It's too early to say.' The inspector looked back at Doris. 'Why do you want protection anyway? Do you have reason to think he will come back? Perhaps you *do* know who it was? Or perhaps you know what he was looking for?'

'I am hiding nothing from you, Chief Inspector.' There was a change in her voice. She seemed gripped with anxiety. 'I am asking for your help. I am frightened.'

'The incident has really shaken Mrs Hornsby up,' said the nurse.

'I understand that,' said Blizzard. He softened his tone. 'But the odds are that, having been disturbed, this is the last place the burglar will want to visit again. I'll make sure uniform keep an extra eye on the village. It's the best I can do and I'll send a detective constable round to take a statement from you.'

'I am not going to talk to a constable!' exclaimed Doris. 'Like I said to Mr Gordon–'

'Yes, well Mr Gordon is no longer here, is he?' Blizzard headed out into the hall. 'I decide who investigates crimes now. Good day to you, Mrs Hornsby.'

With immense relief, the detectives headed outside into the fresh air, away from the fug of the gas fire and the oppressive gloom of the darkened living room. Blinking slightly in the bright sunlight, Blizzard paused to sit on the low front wall for a moment or two and mop his perspiring brow with his sodden handkerchief.

'You OK?' asked Colley.

'It was bloody hot in there.'

'Certainly was,' said Colley. He glanced back at the cottage. 'Do you think it was The Latch Man then? It sounds like his MO.'

'Not sure.' Blizzard stood up and shoved the handkerchief into his trouser pocket. 'I would have said from what we know of him that he's too good to get caught like that.'

'Everyone makes a mistake eventually,' replied Colley as they walked to the car. 'If it is him, this is the first time he has let himself be seen.'

'It still doesn't give us much to go on,' said Blizzard. He got into the car, started the engine and turned the air conditioning on full blast.

'Did you get the impression that Doris knew more than she was letting on?' asked Colley. He got into the vehicle and grimaced at the hot seat. 'When you asked her if she recognised the intruder, she seemed to go a bit funny. And she did seem pretty frightened.'

'You would be if you'd been burgled, David. Besides, for the moment, we have more important things to sort right now.'

'Like what?' asked Colley.

'I noticed that the village shop sells ice cream…'

* * *

An hour later, Doris Hornsby was sitting on her bed, eying the slim brunette standing before her with disapproval.

'And how long have you been a detective constable?' she asked.

'Seven months,' replied Sarah Allatt.

Doris Hornsby snorted her disgust.

Chapter three

It was just after 5.30 the next morning when the police patrol spotted the white van parked on the side of the road leading to the Rotterdam ferry terminal. Two men were changing a rear tyre and, as the patrol vehicle slowed down, one of them glanced over at the officers. He gave them a wave but something about his uneasy demeanour alerted the officer driving the car.

'That doesn't look right,' he said.

His colleague nodded and the driver pulled his vehicle up alongside the van, got out and walked up to the men.

'Won't be long,' said the man who had waved. He spoke English. 'Picked up a puncture. Just about done.'

'Can I see your documents, please?' asked the officer.

'Why do you want to see our documents?'

The officer noted that the man looked increasingly nervous and that sweat was glistening on his brow.

'It's just routine,' said the officer.

'We haven't done anything wrong.'

'Nevertheless, I'd still like to see your…'

The officer's voice tailed off as a third man emerged from the van carrying a handgun, which he pointed at the officer.

'What the–' said the officer.

'Just back off,' said the man.

He gestured for the officers to move back to their vehicle and he and his friends climbed hurriedly back into the van. Hearts pounding and pulses racing, the officers watched in silence as the vehicle drove off, the rear wheel wobbling alarmingly.

'They won't get far,' said the driver when he felt able to speak.

* * *

With the heat already beginning to rise again in Abbey Road Police Station, John Blizzard was walking along the corridor when a dark-haired young woman approached him from the other direction. The inspector smiled a welcome at Sarah Allatt.

'How did it go with Doris Hornsby yesterday?' he asked. 'Did you get her statement OK?'

The detective constable gave him a rueful look.

'Only after a lecture on the folly of youth,' she said. 'And she kept mentioning some fellow called Gordon.'

Blizzard chuckled and continued on his way towards the detective superintendent's office. Five minutes later, he and Arthur Ronald were sitting at the desk, cradling mugs of tea.

'So, was it The Latch Man again?' asked Ronald.

'Sounds like it,' said Blizzard. He frowned. 'Just not like him to get caught out like that. Bit of a schoolboy error.'

Ronald nodded. A pudgy, balding man with ruddy cheeks and eyes with bags which sagged darkly, he had been one of Blizzard's friends for years, the two having first worked together as rookie uniform officers before being reunited at Abbey Road when Ronald assumed command of CID in the area that included Western Division. It had not been a popular decision with some of the senior officers who had fallen foul of Blizzard's tongue down the years but Ronald had insisted and the tumbling crime figures since the appointment had proved the wisdom of his instincts.

'Yes, well, I'm getting flak from all sides,' said the superintendent. 'The old folk in the villages are scared witless and one of the women he burgled is the mother of a magistrate who has complained to the chief. We need to make some progress on this one, John.'

'I know, I know,' sighed Blizzard. 'We're doing everything we can.'

It was not the first time that they had had the same conversation. The Latch Man had prowled the villages to the west of the city for two months. A consummate professional who left no evidence behind for the forensics teams, he targeted houses owned by elderly people living alone, usually women, and would always leave the front door unlocked and on the latch, hence the nickname which police had given him and which had been picked up gleefully by the media.

'So where is David with the investigation?' asked Ronald. He gave Blizzard a hard look. 'I can't help feel that we are dragging our feet on this one.'

'He's doing all he can, Arthur, but he's still no further on, I am afraid. He's had everyone talking to their informants, but nobody seems to know anything. Whoever this guy is, he's working alone, that's for sure.'

'But he must be fencing the gear off to someone.' Ronald took a sip of tea and uncharacteristically loosened his tie as the heat continued to rise and the storm clouds gathered outside.

'You'd think.'

'Look, we need this character off the streets.'

'I know,' said Blizzard. He took a sip of tea. 'But it's taking up a lot of manpower and our resources are stretched pretty thin, as it is. Do you know how many murders we have had on our patch in the past three months? Nine. They don't solve themselves, you know.'

'I thought you'd been telling everyone that they do,' said Ronald, giving him a sly look.

'Yes, but they still generate a lot of paperwork, don't they? Besides, I thought you wanted that budget report writing.' Blizzard looked at Ronald with a gleam in his eye. 'Now, if someone else was to write it for me. Perhaps someone in the Finance Department could–'

'Nice try, John, but no. Just make sure that we do not take our eye off the ball on The Latch Man. We have to reassure the community that we are doing everything we can to catch him.'

'Yeah, OK.' Blizzard knew that his friend was right. The inspector drained his mug. 'Is that what you wanted to see me about?'

'No.' Ronald slid a piece of paper across the desk. 'This has come in from the police in Rotterdam. One of the guys pulled a gun. The wheel fell off the van a mile down the road and they legged it.'

'Where do we come into it?' asked Blizzard, scanning the report.

'Says down the bottom. Final paragraph. The van was booked on to the early morning ferry to Hafton.'

'What else do we know?'

'Nothing really,' said Ronald. 'Not much in the way of descriptions and forensics came up with nothing of note. The plates on the van are fake, as was the name they used to buy the ferry ticket.'

'Intriguing.'

'More than that if they're heading our way and prepared to pull a gun on police officers. Put the word out, will you? See if we can turn anything up. The Dutch are talking about maybe sending someone over if we do.'

'I'll get the boys and girls onto it right away.' Blizzard stood up and headed for the door. 'Although it's all pretty vague.'

'Which is why I don't want you diverting too much manpower away from the Latch Man investigation. That has to be our number one priority, John. The last thing we want is him hurting one of these old dears.'

'I wouldn't worry about that. There's no evidence to suggest he's dangerous.'

'I hope you're right,' said Ronald.

Outside, the first clap of thunder sounded. Distant but loud for all that – making them both jump. Blizzard glanced out of the window at the darkening sky and experienced an uneasy feeling.

'So do I,' he said.

Chapter four

Had she still possessed the power of speech, Edith Bradley would have disagreed with the chief inspector's contention that The Latch Man was not dangerous. However, Edith Bradley was dead, her skull fractured by a heavy blow during a murderous attack at her home in the village of Scawby, two miles from Caitby Mallard, a week after Blizzard's conversation with the superintendent.

It was a neighbour who found the ninety-two-year-old's body, having arrived at the cottage shortly after 9am for her daily check on her elderly friend and discovered the front door unlocked. Pushing the door open tentatively, the neighbour entered the cottage, finding the downstairs dark and deserted, with the curtains closed.

'Edith?' she called.

Her voice seemed to echo round the house and, overwhelmed by dread, the neighbour edged her way slowly up the stairs and entered the bedroom, where she found the old lady. Horrified by what she had seen, she ran downstairs and sat for several minutes in the living room before lifting the phone receiver with a shaking hand and blurting out her story to the police. Then she fled the cottage.

John Blizzard arrived shortly after 9.40, having driven grim-faced along the country roads beneath overcast, rain-filled skies. He parked the car and walked towards the cottage. As he did so, he noticed a small knot of mainly elderly people gathered at the far end of the lane, kept away by police tape. Many of them were crying. The inspector pushed open the front gate. Colley was standing at the front door.

'What have we got, David?' asked the inspector.

'Neighbour says that she was definitely alive at six o'clock last night,' said the sergeant as he led the way into the hall. 'Saw her in her back garden, bringing in the washing before the storm.'

'And you think it's definitely The Latch Man?'

'Yeah. It's not the first time he has been here either. One of his early jobs was in a house over on the Green – took ten thousand quid's worth of jewellery from an old dear's house.'

'Where's the body?'

'Upstairs – it's not pretty, guv. So much for your idea that he is not dangerous.'

Blizzard looked at him sharply but said nothing. The old timbers creaked as they ascended the stairs and entered the darkened bedroom, the curtains still drawn. Edith Bradley lay sprawled grotesquely across the bed, her thinning white hair matted with dried blood, one eye closed and gashed, the other staring lifelessly at the ceiling, the nose bent at a sickening angle and her jaw hanging loose. Her arms, thin and stick-like with age, were half-raised as if the frail old woman had made pathetic attempts to defend herself against the savage onslaught.

'Jesus Christ,' said Blizzard. He wrinkled his nose as the stench of death hit him.

'He gave her a real beating, alright,' said Colley.

There was a sound at the door and they turned to see Detective Inspector Graham Ross, head of forensics in

Western Division, dressed in a white overall. He gestured towards the landing.

'Stay back, please, gents,' he said.

The detectives walked back to the doorway.

'Didn't give her much chance, did he?' said Blizzard. 'Anything missing?'

He gestured at the oak chest of drawers – atop of which were several family photographs – the wardrobe, and the chair over which Edith had carefully draped her clothes for the morning.

'Not sure yet,' said Colley. 'We're struggling to track down any family.'

'Any initial thoughts, Versace?' asked Blizzard, looking at Ross.

'Only that if it is The Latch Man, he normally does not give us much to go on.'

'*If* it's him.'

Ross and Colley looked at the inspector in surprise.

'Come on, guv,' said the sergeant. 'It has all the hallmarks.'

'Yes, it does, but this is a man who gets disturbed in the middle of the night and gives a little bow before leaving. Are we really saying that in the space of a few days he can go from Raffles the gentleman thief to something out of Psycho?'

Blizzard nodded towards the body.

'I mean,' he said, 'this is someone who lost control – not someone as cool and calm as The Latch Man.'

'He's got a point,' said Ross.

'But the front door,' said the sergeant. 'It was left open. Like all the others.'

'Yeah, but since the press office let it slip that we were calling him The Latch Man, everyone knows his signature,' said Blizzard.

The officers recalled Blizzard's anger when an inexperienced stand-in press officer had inadvertently told the local evening paper's crime reporter about the unlocked front doors and the front page of the next day's paper bore the words *Police seek The Latch Man* in large print. The inspector had wanted to keep it quiet: always keep something back so when an arrested person reveals knowledge of it, they cannot claim to have seen it in the media. Rule One. He had been furious at the slip.

'So, you think that we could have a copycat?' said Ross.

'It's a possibility,' replied Blizzard.

'Not sure I buy that,' said Colley. 'Look at the evidence: same area, same kind of cottage, same kind of victim, door left on the latch. It sounds like him to me.'

'I think it's meant to,' said Blizzard. 'If I am wrong, you can tell me so as many times as you want. Can you start things off here, please, David? I want to know absolutely everything about Edith Bradley. Had she lived here long?'

'She was born in the cottage. Never moved.'

'In which case, folks must know everything about her. And work fast, I want a briefing in the squad room at eleven.'

Blizzard had just reached his car when a couple of elderly women standing nearby gestured for him to come over.

'You're DCI Blizzard, aren't you?' asked one of them.

'I am.'

'Is Edith dead?'

'I am afraid she is, yes.'

'We asked the police for more protection after the last break-in,' said the elderly woman. 'You knew that we were scared.'

'We've increased patrols in the villages.'

'Well, we haven't seen them. And now Edith is dead.' The woman's tone of voice was harsh. Accusatory. 'What have you got to say to that, Chief Inspector?'

Blizzard glanced back towards the cottage but said nothing. He was not sure that he could find the right words. And the words that did come into his mind had been uttered by someone else. By Arthur Ronald the previous week. *Just make sure that we do not take our eye off the ball.* Blizzard looked back at the cottage and sighed; he had an awful feeling that they had.

Chapter five

There was a sombre atmosphere in the CID room at Abbey Road Station later that morning. Blizzard stood next to Ronald at the front, looking out at the gathering of officers. Among them was Detective Inspector Chris Ramsey, a dour man in his thirties, slim and tall with short-cropped brown hair, an angular face and a prominent nose. Next to him sat Graham Ross, dressed immaculately in a pressed grey suit with a red silk tie and with his brown wavy hair beautifully groomed as usual. Also among the assembled officers was Sarah Allatt, the squad's most recent arrival, who was relishing the atmosphere of a major investigation.

'OK,' said Blizzard, 'let's make a start. We'll assume that David has been held up. As you all know, an elderly lady was murdered in Scawby this morning. Now… ah, Sergeant, how kind of you to pop into our little gathering.'

Colley held up an apologetic hand.

'Sorry, guv,' he said. The sergeant assumed his customary position leaning against the wall. 'Got chatting to some old dears over tea and biscuits. It's a dangerous job but somebody has to do it.'

There was a murmur of laughter.

'Did you get anything?' asked Blizzard.

'A nice recipe for sponge cake. It's all in the eggs, apparently.'

'Apart from that?'

'Only that Edith Bradley was a harmless little old lady getting on quietly with life,' said Colley. He glanced down at his pocketbook. 'A widow for many years. Hubby worked for the council. Her main interests were the bridge club and Scawby Gardening Circle. Won Best Kept Garden two years ago.'

'Not much to go on there,' said Blizzard.

'You'd think.' There was a gleam in Colley's eyes. 'Except that, rather like Doris Hornsby, Edith Bradley was not exactly untainted by the ways of the criminal underworld.'

'What does that mean?' asked Blizzard.

'Her son was one Anthony Bradley.'

'Bradley, Bradley,' said Blizzard. His brow furrowed as he tried to remember the name.

'Better known as Tony. Worked for…'

Recognition dawned as Blizzard dragged the memory from the recesses of his mind. The same recognition had just hit Arthur Ronald, who clicked his fingers.

'George Leys,' he said. 'He worked for him back in the day.'

'Of course,' said Blizzard. 'He was the gang's enforcer, wasn't he, Arthur?'

'He was indeed. Him and Eric Leys did the heavy stuff. They fled the city together after George was killed. Not sure how it helps us, mind. Tony is long dead.'

'As is Eric,' said Colley. 'They died in the same car crash. Went off the road in the Costa del Sol one night. Driving too fast, hit a tree. But, interestingly enough, they are not the only connection between Edith and Doris. One of the neighbours said that until about a year and a half ago, one of Edith's regular visitors was Doris Hornsby. They used to have afternoon tea two or three times a year.'

'Boy, wouldn't you have liked to be a fly on that wall?' said Blizzard. 'Do we know why they stopped seeing each other?'

'Edith told friends that it was Doris who brought things to a halt. Told Edith that her son did not like them meeting. Martin did not appreciate the way it reminded him of the bad old days, apparently. God knows why, it's not like the old girls were planning anything – unless they were going to use Edith's motorised scooter as a getaway vehicle.'

Laughter rippled round the room. Blizzard waited for it to die away.

'Do we know anything else?' he asked.

'Struggling really. Tony was Edith's only child and no one knows if there are any other relatives who can help fill in the gaps. There's talk of a distant cousin in Canada but that's about it.'

'What about forensics?' asked the inspector. He looked at Ross. 'Anything useful there, Versace?'

'Usual story, I am afraid. The place is clean as a whistle. That's why I'm pretty sure it must be The Latch Man.'

'Possibly,' said Blizzard. 'Although, the link with Doris Hornsby is well worth pursuing.'

'It's probably just coincidence,' said Ronald. 'A couple of old dears having tea and scones. By all means bear it in mind, John, but I can't really see what good digging up history is going to do us. And if the media get hold of it, it'll be a distraction we could well do without. They're already in over-drive.'

'Nevertheless, I don't think we should discount it. Not yet, anyway.' Blizzard noticed the sceptical looks on several faces in the room, including that of Colley. 'And I'm not convinced that the murder is the work of The Latch Man either. I think we may be jumping to conclusions far too quickly by going straight for the panicky burglar theory.'

Every face in the room was turned to Ronald to see his reaction; the superintendent said nothing but his lips were pursed as the two friends stared at each other.

'I could always be wrong, mind,' said Blizzard. He opted for the diplomatic approach. 'Can't recall when it has ever happened, but I I'm sure it has. In fact, now I think of it, it did happen once… back in 2002, I think it was. November. Back end of the month.'

The comment eased the tension and there were relieved smiles from the gathering. Everyone knew that investigation teams prized unity above all things and Ronald nodded his appreciation at the gesture. Besides, Blizzard's hunches had been right too many times to be dismissed lightly.

'So, what now?' asked Ronald.

'I want us to go back to Scawby and keep digging,' said Blizzard. 'Maybe someone saw something they have not told us. And there's bound to be folks we haven't talked to yet. David, I want you to keep on top of that.'

Colley nodded.

'And,' continued Blizzard, 'I want us to go back to our informants as well. I know we've done it already but the murder may change things. Arthur's right, The Latch Man must be fencing his stuff somewhere. We'll do a deal with him, if we have to, but run it past me or the Super first.'

He glanced at Ronald, who nodded.

'Sarah,' said Blizzard, looking at Allatt. 'I want you to go back to Doris Hornsby–'

'Do I have to?' she asked plaintively.

'I know she gave you an ear-bashing last time, and I appreciate it may be a long shot, but I want to find out more about the links between her and Edith.'

'Yes, guv,' she said glumly.

'Chris,' said Blizzard, turning to Ramsey, 'I know we have a lot on at the moment but we are going to need more bodies for this one. Free up who you can, will you?'

'We may need overtime,' warned the DI.

'Run it past me first,' said Ronald. He gave Blizzard a look. 'I have been getting some flak about how much we are spending and it does not help that a certain chief inspector is late with his budget report...'

'You love me really,' said Blizzard.

* * *

An hour later, Sarah Allatt was walking towards Doris Hornsby's house in Caitby Mallard when she saw the vicar standing at the entrance to the parish church. He quickly turned away but something about his reaction alerted the constable's instincts. She pushed her way through the gate and walked up the path.

'Reverend Sparks?' she said and produced her warrant card. 'DC Allatt, Western CID.'

'I wondered if you'd come to see me,' said the vicar. He sighed. 'Nasty business. May she rest in peace. Mind, I'm not sure that's likely with everything that's been going on. All the tension in that house can't have helped.'

'What do you mean?'

'Well, the unpleasantness in the church, of course. Not often you get people coming to blows at a funeral, is it?'

'I'm not sure we're talking about the same thing,' said the constable. 'I am making enquiries into the murder of Edith Bradley at Scawby. Who are you talking about…?'

Chapter six

John Blizzard had some hard thinking to do as he sat in his office early that afternoon, sifting through initial reports from his officers engaged on the murder investigation. The heat had returned with a vengeance and the chief inspector was sweating profusely as the temperature rose. He glanced down at the photographs of the old lady's battered face and frowned. Was he wrong? Was the simple truth that The Latch Man lost control when Edith Bradley disturbed him? Blizzard glanced at the grisly pictures again, thought of the bow that The Latch Man had given when he was seen by Doris Hornsby and shook his head.

His reverie was interrupted when a bright-eyed Sarah Allatt rushed into the office without knocking.

'Guv!' she exclaimed breathlessly. 'She's dead!'

'Pray, who is dead?' asked Blizzard.

'Doris Hornsby!'

'Really?' Blizzard motioned to the chair. 'Do tell me more.'

'I went to see her again, like you said,' said the young constable as she sat down. 'But on the way, I bumped into the vicar. He said that Doris died in her sleep a couple of days after you saw her.'

'When's the funeral? I might pop along to see which of the old timers come out of the woodwork. Should be a who's who of villainy.'

'Well, that's the thing. It was held yesterday.'

'Yesterday?' said Blizzard. His suspicions were aroused. 'That's remarkably quick.'

'That's what I thought and so does the vicar. I think he wanted someone to talk to, actually. It all came pouring out.'

'What came pouring out?'

'The way it was handled by her son. Martin did not even put a death notice in the paper or tell the rest of the family – or any of the friends and neighbours – when the funeral was being held. He wanted it kept private. They only found out from the vicar.'

'I assume Martin was not impressed?'

'Had a real go at the vicar for telling folks. The vicar says that it's typical of him. He reckons that people were really upset. The neighbours had done chores for her for years, brought her shopping in, that sort of thing – and they wanted to pay their last respects but Martin refused to talk to them. He even refused to let the nurse in. She was in tears, apparently.'

'Intriguing.'

'It had been like this for months,' said Allatt. 'Like Martin was wrapping his mother in a cocoon, according to the vicar.'

'So, I take it no one went to the funeral?'

'Some of them turned up at the church. There was a bit of a scene with Martin's niece and nephew.'

'I didn't know that Eric had children.'

'Well, he did.' She glanced down at her notebook. 'Janice Poulter and Robert Leys. There was an argument when the hearse arrived. Robert pushed Martin when he tried to stop folks entering the church. The neighbours reckon Martin was lucky not to get his lights punched out. The vicar had to appeal for calm.'

'I'm not surprised.'

'According to the vicar, they were arguing about the will. The cottage alone is worth £450,000 and Doris's husband left her a lot of money as well. Everyone assumed that she would leave something to members of the family but she changed the will so that it all went to Martin.'

'Fascinating stuff,' said Blizzard. 'And do we know what killed Doris?'

'Martin told neighbours that it was natural causes and warned them to keep their noses out of his affairs. Threatened to call in his solicitor if they bothered him again.'

'She's been cremated, I assume?'

'Buried at the parish church.'

'Surprised there was anywhere to put her.' Blizzard recalled the churchyard with its crumbling old stones packed tightly together amid the overgrown vegetation. 'I thought they closed it for burials years ago.'

'They did and the vicar told her that but Doris wanted to be buried next to her first husband. She insisted.'

'Typical Doris,' said Blizzard with a low laugh. 'She's faced down tougher characters than the Lord's ambassador on Earth, has Doris.'

'Martin tried to get the decision overturned so that she could be cremated but the vicar refused. Said he had to respect her last wishes.'

'Definitely something funny going on there, Sarah. I want you to go back to Caitby Mallard. Talk to the neighbours and the vicar, get it all down in statements. I think it's time to see the grandchildren.'

'Do you want me to do that as well?' she asked.

'No, I'll go with David.' Blizzard gave her a reassuring smile on seeing her disappointed expression. 'Don't worry, I won't cut you out. You're part of the team.'

She headed for the door, still looking unconvinced.

'Oh, Constable,' said Blizzard.

She turned to look at him.

'Good work,' he said.

The smile lit up her face.

'Who says I can't man-manage?' murmured Blizzard when she had gone.

A few moments later he looked up to see Colley entering the office.

'Sarah been to see you?' asked the sergeant.

'Yeah, she's just left.'

'Interesting enough for you?'

'More than that.' Blizzard stood up and grabbed his jacket. 'I know you're not sure if it's relevant to the death of Edith Bradley but it's definitely worth checking out, I would say. Come on, time to play happy families.'

As they headed out of the office, Chris Ramsey approached them down the corridor.

'Ah, Chris,' said Blizzard. 'Just the person. Arthur was asking me if we'd turned up anything on that request from the police in Rotterdam?'

'Nothing, I am afraid, guv. We've checked all our informants but we've not come up with anything. If the guys are from Hafton, no one knows about it or who they are.'

'Yeah, same here,' said Colley. 'Blank faces all round. If you ask me, it's a bum steer. Our Dutch pals smoking too much of the wacky baccy.'

'You're probably right,' said Blizzard. However, somewhere at the back of his brain a warning bell was ringing.

* * *

Shortly after 3pm, the Transit van carrying three men rumbled up the ramp which led from the ferry into the main terminal at the Port of Hafton. Within half an hour, it had passed unchallenged through Customs and headed out onto the dual carriageway leading into the city.

Chapter seven

The clearance of Doris Hornsby's home was well under way when the two detectives arrived. A small knot of grim-faced neighbours had gathered a few yards further down the lane and were watching in tense silence as two scruffy men in jeans and T-shirts ferried items to their van parked outside the cottage.

'There's definitely a rabbit away here,' muttered Blizzard as they pushed their way through the front gate.

'Too right,' said Colley.

Martin Hornsby, who was standing on the doorstep, glared at them as they approached. A tall, slim man with greying hair and dressed in shirt and tie and grey slacks, the manner in which he viewed them through narrowed eyes betrayed the hostility that he felt at their arrival.

'This is private property,' he said. 'Whoever you are, you have no right to be here. Please leave immediately or I will call the police.'

Blizzard smiled thinly; he loved it when people said that.

'We are the police,' he said. He fished his warrant card out of his jacket pocket. 'And we have every right to be here, Mr Hornsby. Every right.'

'What would the police want here?'

Hornsby's voice was defiant, the irritation tempered by discretion, but the detectives thought they also sensed a touch of unease beneath the bravado.

'We'd rather explain it inside,' said Blizzard.

Reluctantly, Hornsby stood aside.

'Go into the living room,' he said.

Blizzard led the way into the empty front room, followed by Hornsby.

'Shall we sit down?' asked Blizzard. 'Ah, no, all the chairs seem to have gone. You certainly do not waste much time, do you, Mr Hornsby. Or should that be Mr Leys? I am never quite sure.'

'Hornsby. I don't use the name Leys.'

'Too many bad connotations, I suppose. Being the son of a villain was not exactly a great image to have in the accountancy business, I imagine. Although from my dealings with accountants down the years…'

Blizzard did not finish the sentence. Hornsby glared at him again.

'Anyway,' said Blizzard. 'My name is Detective Chief Inspec–'

'I don't care who you are, why are you here? The last thing I need is the police poking their noses in when they are not needed. My mother died a natural death.'

'I imagine that to be the case, but we still have a few questions. Purely routine and I hate to intrude at this time of grief.'

The inspector's words were the appropriate ones but his tone of voice suggested that he did not mean them and Martin Hornsby knew it.

'Be quick about it and be on your way,' he snapped. 'I am rather busy.'

'You certainly are,' replied Blizzard. He glanced out into the hallway at the clearance men struggling down the stairs with a chest of drawers. The inspector winced at the splintering sound as they banged it against the wall. 'You don't let the grass grow under your feet, do you? Or over your mother's grave, for that matter.'

'That is out of order, Chief Inspector!' Hornsby took a step towards him. 'Why are you here?'

'Did you know that a day or so before she died, your mother called us in because she had been burgled?'

'No, she hadn't. She imagined it all. I told her that.'

'She seemed pretty certain,' said Colley. He grimaced as the clearance men dropped the chest of drawers on the drive.

'Be careful!' shouted Hornsby. He pushed past the detectives and out onto the drive where the men were trying to pick the piece of furniture up again. 'That could be worth money down the saleroom!'

'Grief certainly does take many forms,' said Blizzard.

Colley gave a low laugh. Hornsby heard it as he walked back into the living room but, because he had been unable to make out the comment, he said nothing.

'As a matter of interest, where did you get Laurel and Hardy?' asked Colley as the men started to load the chest of drawers into their van.

'That is none of your business.'

'If we could return to your mother,' said Blizzard. 'We took her story about the burglar seriously, even if you didn't.'

'Then more fool you, Chief Inspector. That nurse stuffed so many pills in her that my mother didn't know where she was half the time. And all that rubbish about him bowing to her.'

'Your mother did not come over as confused to us. She seemed very clear in her mind. Then a few days after that incident, your mother's old friend Edith Bradley is murdered by an intruder.'

'I know nothing about that.'

'Be that as it may,' said Blizzard, 'am I not right in thinking that your brother and her son were members of the same gang? Your father's gang, indeed.'

'That's got nothing to do with me,' said Hornsby. He was more guarded now. 'I disapproved of what they did and well you know it. And if this is about them, might I remind you that Eric is long dead. As is that thug Bradley. If you continue with this line of questioning, Chief Inspector, I will lodge a complaint of harassment against–'

'I'll put it with all the others. You see, it did strike us as odd that two elderly ladies, both friends, both with family connections to organised crime, both burgled – possibly by the same man – have both ended up dead.'

'My mother died of natural causes,' repeated Hornsby.

'Did a doctor certify that?' asked Colley.

Hornsby looked at him for several seconds. They could see the thought processes going on behind the eyes. He seemed uneasy, rattled.

'Yes, he did,' he said at length.

'And could we see the death certificate?'

'You'll need a warrant.'

'Actually, we don't but it would save us time if–'

'I have no desire to help you, Sergeant.'

'Why so secretive, Mr Hornsby?' asked Colley. 'A quick look at the certificate and all this would be cleared up.'

'Family matters should not be of any interest to anyone.' Hornsby gestured through the front window at the gaggle of curious neighbours who had edged a little closer to the cottage. 'Look at them. Vultures, all of them. All they want is her money.'

'They seem pretty decent people,' said Blizzard. 'And did not a number of them keep an eye on your mother in her later years?'

'Busybodies, that's what they are,' said Hornsby. He walked out into the hall. 'Always poking their noses into her affairs.'

'Until you cut them out of her life, that is,' said Blizzard, following him. 'Now why would you do a thing like that? They only wanted to help. And why was your mother buried so quickly?'

The inspector stood aside as the perspiring clearance men headed back up the stairs. He smiled thinly as he recognised one of them. The chief inspector nodded at Colley, who grinned.

'Isn't that Terry Hibbs?' asked Blizzard, loud enough for the clearance man to hear.

'Yeah, we nicked him for handling stolen goods a couple of years ago,' said Colley as Hibbs scuttled up the stairs. 'House clearance of a sort, I suppose.'

'Antiques, wasn't it?'

'Sure was. From an elderly widow, as I recall.'

Hornsby looked alarmed but said nothing.

'So,' said Blizzard, returning to his theme, 'why did you have your mother buried so quickly, Mr Hornsby? And why have this place cleared so soon? She has only been dead a few days.'

'Why wait? This has been a difficult enough time without having to prolong it. I was very close to my mother and I wanted to get the funeral over and done with.'

'Ah, yes, the funeral. I understand there was some unpleasantness with members of the family. May I ask why you were so insistent that your mother be cremated?'

Hornsby was about to reply when two men walked up the drive, carrying a *For Sale* sign.

'By the gate alright, mate?' one of them asked as Hornsby walked to the front door.

Hornsby nodded and the men started hammering the sign into the ground.

'You do seem to be rushing into–' began Blizzard.

'Look,' exclaimed Hornsby furiously. 'I am sick of all these insinuations! If you want to ask me anything else, you will have to arrest me – and, somehow, I can't see you doing that. This is nothing more than a fishing expedition and I demand that you leave this property immediately.'

For a moment, it seemed as if Blizzard would refuse the request but, after a pause, he turned on his heel and stalked out of the cottage. Colley followed him down the path and the group of neighbours separated to let them through to their car. The number of people had swelled and Blizzard saw that Sarah Allatt was now among them.

'They want to talk to you,' said the constable.

'What about?' asked Blizzard.

'Did he murder her?' asked one of the neighbours as the inspector unlocked the vehicle.

Blizzard surveyed the speaker for a few moments. She was a bright-eyed, intelligent-looking woman in her early sixties with grey hair beginning to streak the blonde locks which poked out from beneath a battered green floppy hat. She was holding a pair of secateurs, which she slipped into her apron pocket.

'Marion Rowbotham,' she said and extended a mud-caked hand. 'Sorry about the dirt. I've been gardening. In fact, I used to look after Doris's garden for her.'

Blizzard declined to shake the hand.

'And why would you think that he murdered her?' he asked instead.

'Isn't that why you are here?'

'We are merely carrying out routine inquiries.'

'Hardly routine if someone like you is here. You're John Blizzard, aren't you? I've seen your picture in the newspaper. It must be something important for you to be involved.'

'And do you have any evidence that she was murdered?'

'No, but–'

'Then I would suggest that you refrain from spreading wild rumours,' said the inspector.

Marion Rowbotham looked as if she were about to speak before the fierce look on the detective's face changed her mind and she stayed silent.

'That goes for all of you,' said Blizzard. He gave the neighbours a stern look. 'I have no time – no time – for groundless gossip in situations like this. Do I make myself absolutely clear?'

They nodded and the inspector got into his car without a further word. He did not speak as he drove the detectives back out of the village either. It was only when they were in the country lanes again that Colley glanced over at his boss.

'What are you thinking, guv?' he asked.

'I am thinking,' said Blizzard, 'that I want to know every bit of groundless gossip that is circulating in Caitby Mallard.'

Colley chuckled.

'Of course, you do,' he said.

Blizzard had just returned to his office at Abbey Road when Arthur Ronald walked into the room.

'A word in your shell-like,' said the superintendent. He took a seat and looked across the desk at Blizzard with a weary expression on his face.

'I can guess what this is about,' said Blizzard. 'Martin Hornsby.'

'His solicitor has just been on the phone, threatening to serve us with an injunction if you continue to harass his client.'

'That didn't take long.'

'I warned you about digging up past history, John. You have no evidence that Doris died of anything but natural causes or that there's any link with the murder of Edith Bradley.'

'Are you warning me off, Arthur?'

'Would you take any notice of me if I did?'

'You're the governor.'

'Sometimes I do wonder.' Ronald gave a half-smile. 'And no, I am not warning you off. You are right, something about this does stink.'

'That's my boy,' said Blizzard.

'Just go carefully,' said Ronald. 'Martin Hornsby is the kind of man who can cause us a lot of trouble.'

* * *

Having set fire to the van on wasteland near Hafton ferry terminal, the three men took a taxi to the sprawling warren of rundown Victorian houses on the edge of Hafton city centre. The cab pulled up half-way along Louisa Street where they got out, paid the driver and walked the rest of the way to one of the houses. When one of them hammered on the door, it was opened by a young man in jeans, T-shirt and a baseball cap.

'You got through then,' he said as he opened the door wide to let them in. His voice was respectful. Reverential almost. 'Good trip?'

The three men brushed past him without speaking.

Chapter eight

Blizzard and Colley had not seen the last of Marion Rowbotham that day because, when they met Eric Leys' children that evening, she was in the living room of the semi-detached house owned by his daughter, not far from Abbey Road Police Station. A slim, attractive divorcee with short reddish hair and freckled features, Janice Poulter was dressed in a black T-shirt and jeans and smiled at them as she handed round mugs of tea. There was no such welcome from her brother. A motor mechanic, Robert Leys had come straight from work and was still dressed in blue overalls. The detectives immediately took a dislike to him with his greasy short brown hair, his squat features and his nose bent out of shape by a schooldays fight. A front tooth was chipped, a legacy of another brawl. It was what jogged Colley's memory.

'We have met before, have we not?' said the sergeant.

'Might have.' The reply was guarded.

'Yeah, five years ago. You attacked a bouncer. You were lucky just to get six months. That bloke was off work for the best part of a year.'

'I was going through a difficult time, what, with my divorce and that.'

'You'd gone through twelve pints as well – and you had been taking uppers.'

'I ain't been on the drugs since then and I ain't been in bother since I got out of prison neither.'

'Except at your grandmother's funeral,' said Colley.

Robert said nothing and stared down at his stockinged feet; his sister had insisted he take off his dirty boots. It was Marion who broke the silence.

'It was nothing,' she said.

'And pray, why are you here?' asked Blizzard. 'You're like rent-a-neighbour.'

'Not a comment that does you justice, Chief Inspector.'

'People keep telling me that,' said Blizzard.

He surveyed her for a few moments. Having discarded her gardening clothes, Marion was dressed in a pleated green skirt and a yellow blouse, over which, despite the closeness of the evening, she wore a thin yellow cardigan. The image was calm, refined, the assurance of a woman who, before her retirement, had spent more than thirty years teaching school pupils and was fazed by little in life, including police officers perspiring in the clammy early evening heat.

'And in answer to your question,' she said, 'I am here because I am a family friend.'

'She is,' said Janice. She reached out a hand to touch her lightly on the arm. 'We are very grateful to her. She has kept us in touch with Granny.'

'You didn't see her yourself?' asked Blizzard.

'We used to.' Janice smiled wistfully at the memory. 'I used to go over there a couple of times a month – she loved to see the children, they played in her garden. They loved searching for the snails behind the greenhouse. And they loved Granny to bits.'

Janice raised her eyes to the ceiling as there was a loud thump from upstairs.

'That's the kids now,' she said.

‘Sounds like a herd of elephants,’ said Blizzard. His comment was not meant unkindly and the tense atmosphere relaxed a little.

‘How old are they?’ asked Colley. He winced as another loud crash emanated from one of the bedrooms.

‘Five and seven, going on fifty-seven,’ said Janice. She gave the officers an apologetic look. ‘They’re supposed to be drawing quietly.’

‘My daughter’s the same, a few years younger, mind.’ Colley glanced at Blizzard, whose son was not yet one. ‘You’ve got all this to come.’

There was another loud crash.

‘I’ll go,’ said Marion.

‘No,’ said Robert. He stood and gave a lopsided grin, the first time he had abandoned his surly expression. ‘I’ll do it.’

‘Don’t misjudge him,’ said Janice once he had left the room. ‘He’s just a bit funny about policemen. He has tried so hard to get his life together and keep out of trouble. He’s a decent man, really he is.’

From upstairs, there came peals of laughter from the children.

‘They love their Uncle Robbie,’ said Janice. ‘And he dotes on them. There isn’t anything he would not do for them.’

A few moments later he was back, smiling as he entered the room but having restored his suspicious expression by the time he sat down.

‘Thanks, love,’ said Janice affectionately.

‘So, when did the kids last see their grandmother?’ asked Colley.

‘A year ago. Maybe more.’

‘Why so long?’

‘All Martin’s doing,’ said Robert. ‘He’d got his claws into Doris. That bastard turned her against us all.’

'Granny Doris was an independent spirit,' said Janice. 'But last year she announced out of the blue that she did not want to see any of us again. It was a terrible shock.'

'Did she say why?' asked Colley.

'She wouldn't tell us but we knew that it was Martin. He's a manipulative man.' Her voice was laced with anger. 'He'd ignored her for years but, when he heard that she was ill, he was always round the cottage, trying to wheedle his way into her affections.'

'Why do you think that was?' asked the sergeant.

'For her money,' said Robert. 'It's obvious, ain't it?'

'I think it went deeper than that,' said Janice. 'I don't think he could stomach the thought of us getting anything when she died. Martin hated the fact that Dad went into the business with Grandad. I take it you know all about Grandad's business, Chief Inspector?'

'Business is one word for it,' said Blizzard. 'Suffice to say that George Leys was well known to the police.'

'I am sure he was. Anyway, that's when it started.'

'What started?'

'The rift between the brothers. Martin was furious when Dad followed Grandad into crime. They were really close when they were kids but they hardly ever spoke after that – Christmas, birthdays, that was about it. After Grandad was murdered and Dad went to Spain, Martin cut off all contact with us – not that there had been much anyway. He'd never really bothered with us, even when we were kids.'

'But surely he could not blame you for what your Dad did?' said Colley. 'You were only kids at the time.'

'Very moral is our Martin,' said Janice. Her voice was tinged with irony. 'We were the children of Eric Leys and that was enough for him. We see him in the street sometimes, but he always cuts us dead, doesn't he, Rob?'

'Yeah. He brought his car into the garage one day but, when he realised that I worked there, he drove straight out again. Daft bastard.'

'But your grandmother kept up contact with you,' said Blizzard. 'So, what happened a year or so ago that made her change her mind?'

'I can answer that,' said Marion. 'Like Janice says, Martin Hornsby is a manipulative man. Doris was increasingly frail and she'd started to get confused.'

'She seemed sharp enough when we saw her,' said Blizzard.

'I bet if you'd gone back the next day, she wouldn't have remembered talking to you. She went through bouts of forgetting things – leaving the gas on, that kind of thing. I suspected that she might have been in the early stages of Alzheimer's. Martin took his chance. Filled her mind with nonsense.' Marion gestured to Janice and Robert. 'He told her that these two were only after her money.'

'A terrible thing to say,' said Janice bitterly.

'He said the same about us,' added Marion. 'Said her neighbours were–'

'Vultures?' said Blizzard.

'He told you as well then?'

'He did.'

'Typical of the man. Anyway, Doris became more and more introverted and started to turn our help away. She always said Martin or the nurse would do it instead. Whenever I tried to talk to Martin about it, he cut me dead.'

'So was the nurse his idea?' asked Blizzard.

'No,' said Marion. 'Doris hired Annie Meadows herself a few weeks ago. Annie told me that Martin was furious when he found out. Said it was a waste of money but Doris stuck to her guns. She'd been really shaken up by the stories about The Latch Man and one of Annie's jobs was to check all the windows and doors before she went in the evening.'

'So *did* Doris see a burglar in her living room?' asked Blizzard.

'Who knows?' said Marion. 'The nurse could easily have left the front door unlocked by mistake. Would not have been the first time, especially if she'd been at Doris's sherry.'

'So, what happened at the funeral?' asked Colley.

'It was awful,' said Marion. 'When Martin and Myra arrived at the–'

'Myra?'

'His wife. A shrew of a woman. They're as bad as each other. Martin was furious when he saw that fifty or sixty of us had turned up. Half the village was there. Family, friends, neighbours…'

'I even took the kids,' said Janice. 'I wanted them to say goodbye to their granny. Martin was shouting. Said we had no right to be there. The poor vicar did not know what to do, which is when Robert… well, you've probably heard…'

She looked at her brother.

'I may have pushed him in the chest,' said Robert. 'It weren't hard or anything. He just took a step back. He never fell over or anything like that.'

'Some of us did get into the service,' said Janice. 'Martin and Myra sat at the front but they never turned round. They waited in the church office afterwards until the undertaker came to take them home.'

'I take it Doris left everything to Martin?' asked the inspector.

'Apparently,' said Janice. 'We only knew she'd changed her will because the nurse told Marion. I rang Martin a few times to ask if we could see it, but he never rang back. I even went to the cottage but the nurse said Granny did not want to talk to me. Do you think Martin has done something illegal?'

'I'll get back to you on that one.' Blizzard stood up. 'One more thing. Edith Bradley. Did you know her?'

'Granny talked about her sometimes.' Janice gave him an appalled look. 'Surely you do not think Granny's death has anything to do with what happened to poor Edith?'

'I am not sure what to think,' said Blizzard.

Leaving them pondering his words, the detectives left the room. Marion saw them into the hallway. As she opened the front door, she glanced up the stairs where two curly heads had popped round the bannister. There were giggles when Colley winked at them on his way out of the front door.

'It's not right,' said Marion once she and the detectives were walking down the path. 'Doris loved those kids, absolutely loved them.'

She saw them through the gate, gave them a sad look and turned back towards the house.

'So, what do you think?' asked Colley when she was out of earshot.

'I think,' said Blizzard as he unclipped the gate, 'that I want to know exactly what is in Doris Hornsby's will.'

'But even if she did leave everything to Martin, surely it is a civil matter? How can we justify an investigation? I mean there's no sign of a crime and all families have feuds, don't they? Don't look at me like that, it's what Ronald will say.'

'You're getting to sound more and more like him with every passing day,' said Blizzard. He unlocked the car. 'You thinking of going for inspector again?'

'I have got a point, though, haven't I?'

'I know, I know.' Blizzard glanced back at the house before getting into the driver's seat. 'But something really is not right about this and that rankles with me. If anyone kicks up a fuss about us investigating Doris's death, we can say we are trying to find out if the shock of the break-in killed her.'

'Thin. Very thin.'

'I know it is.' Blizzard started the engine. 'But I've justified investigations on less and if you are not prepared–'

'Hey, don't have a go at me! Look, I'll be honest, I thought you were barking up the wrong tree but now' – the sergeant looked thoughtfully back at the house – 'now, I am not so sure.'

'Ah, a prophet in his own land,' said Blizzard. He had a satisfied smile on his face as he slipped the car into first gear and edged it out into the road.

'Why did I know that you were going to say that?'

Half an hour later, Blizzard was wrapping things up for the day when Chris Ramsey walked into his office.

'Been looking for you, guv,' he said. 'The Dutch police have been on again. They've been reviewing CCTV from Rotterdam ferry terminal and reckon those three guys got through today in a different vehicle.'

'The Hafton ferry?'

'Yeah. And a van was found torched over on the East Side. We suspect they may have used that. Versace has talked to the East Side forensics guys but there's nothing of use. Whoever did it, made a good job of it. Sounds like they may be pros. The Dutch police are still thinking of sending someone over.'

The alarm bells sounded ever louder in Blizzard's mind.

Chapter nine

The next morning, Blizzard summoned the nurse to attend Abbey Road Police Station. As the inspector and Colley stared at Annie Meadows across the interview room desk, it was clear that she did not wish to be there. However, behind her surly demeanour, Blizzard sensed an unease. He found himself ever more intrigued.

'What is this about?' asked the nurse.

'We are investigating the murder of Edith Bradley,' said Blizzard.

'What's that got to do with me? I did not know the woman.'

'Yes, but Doris did.'

'That's nothing to do with me,' said Annie. 'I was just her nurse. Besides, they stopped seeing each other a few months before I started working for Doris.'

'Do you know why they stopped seeing each other?'

'No.'

'Come on, Annie,' said Blizzard. 'Doris must have confided in you. You can't work that closely with someone without becoming close.'

'She never mentioned Edith,' said the nurse firmly.

'OK,' said Blizzard. 'Let's try something else then, shall we? Do you know why Doris changed her will?'

'Doris never talked to me about money. I took cheques to the bank from time to time and posted the odd payment for bills for her but that was all.'

'Did you at any time see details of–'

'Why are you asking me these things, Chief Inspector? Doris died of natural causes, what's her money got to do with it?'

'We just want to get things straight in our mind,' said Blizzard. 'Why don't you want to help us?'

'I don't want to be involved. Martin handled all her finances and he doesn't like people talking about his mother's private affairs.'

'So he told us,' said Blizzard. 'Tell me about him. See, we've been told that she changed her will only after he came on the scene and that–'

'Am I under arrest?'

'No, but–'

'So, is there any way you can stop me leaving?'

'Not as–'

The nurse stood up.

'Then I'll bid you good day,' she said. 'Will someone please show me out?'

Blizzard considered remonstrating with her but her resolute expression made him think better of the idea and he nodded. While Colley was taking her to reception, the inspector headed back to his office where he had just sat down when Sarah Allatt knocked on the door.

'How did it go with the solicitor?' asked Blizzard, motioning the young constable into the room.

'Hard work, guv.' Allatt sat down. 'He really didn't want to talk to me. Kept going on about client confidentiality. Said Martin wouldn't like it. I had to threaten him with getting a warrant in the end, like you suggested.'

'Did it work?'

The detective constable placed a series of photocopied sheets on the table.

'That Doris's will?' asked Blizzard, a gleam in his eye.

'It is.'

Blizzard eagerly scanned the contents for a couple of minutes, only looking up as Colley entered the room and took a seat.

'You seen this?' asked Blizzard. He held up the document.

'Sure have,' said the sergeant. 'Makes for good reading, does it not?'

'It certainly does. According to this, everything we've heard is correct. Martin gets the house, investments, savings, the lot.' Blizzard ran a finger down a column of figures. 'The best part of eight hundred thousand. Even minus inheritance tax, it's a tidy sum. Do we know what the previous version said, Sarah?'

'I couldn't get a copy of it, unfortunately. The solicitor said he'd destroyed it.' Allatt looked down at her notebook. 'But according to him, she had intended to share her money round her family and friends, 30 percent to Martin, 20 percent each to Janice and Robert, 15 percent in trust to Janice's children and 15 percent to be divided equally between close friends and neighbours, including the nurse and Marion Rowbotham.'

'She gets everywhere, that woman,' said Blizzard. 'Does the lawyer know why Doris changed the will?'

'She wouldn't tell him but he said he had no reason to challenge it. He reckons that it was her decision and that she had all her marbles when she did it.'

Blizzard glanced back at the figures again.

'It's more than enough to justify murder,' he said.

'Except, the death certificate confirms natural causes,' said Colley. He held up a piece of paper. 'The coroner has just dropped it in. Cause of death, as certified by her GP, was a heart attack. She'd suffered poor circulation for years. No mention of dementia.'

Blizzard sat back in his seat.

'We're missing something,' he said.

'Are you sure?' said Colley.

'Why, aren't you?'

'I'm not, no, guv. For a start–'

Arthur Ronald walked into the office with a grave expression on his face. He looked at Colley and Allatt.

'Can you leave us for a few moments, please?' he said.

When they had gone, the superintendent sat down heavily at the desk and looked unhappily at his friend.

'I very rarely order you to lay off an inquiry, John,' he said. 'I've pretty much given you a free hand since you got the job here but that's what I am telling you to do with Doris Hornsby.'

'Why would you–'

'I understand that you sent Sarah to see the Hornsbys' solicitor?' asked Ronald.

'Yeah, she's just come back.'

'And did she find anything to justify starting a criminal investigation?'

'Not as such, but–'

'Well, the first thing the lawyer did was ring Martin Hornsby, who went ballistic, apparently. The next thing the lawyer did was telephone the force solicitor, threatening to serve an injunction on us if we persist in asking questions about Doris. Said it's all insinuation without any basis.'

'I take it the force solicitor rolled over to have his tummy tickled as usual?'

'He did, yes. Oh, don't look like that, John, he's right on this one, isn't he?'

Blizzard did not reply.

'So, unless we get anything new,' continued Ronald, 'Martin Hornsby is off limits. I know that you've been looking for a case that's a bit more challenging, but this isn't it. It's a distraction when we've got Edith Bradley's murder nowhere near being solved and The Latch Man putting the fear of God into our villages. The Control Room has been inundated with calls from worried old dears since Edith died and the local councillors are demanding answers. I don't blame them.'

'Neither do I, Arthur, but something stinks.'

'It may well do but, as it stands, we have nothing to connect the murder of Edith Bradley with the death of Doris Hornsby, other than they were probably both burgled by the same man, but he's screwed lots of old people's homes. No, Edith has to be our focus. The last thing we want is another old dear being murdered by this lunatic.' Ronald stood up. 'Which is why the chief has told us to hold a press conference here tomorrow morning to offer some reassurance to the public.'

* * *

Still seething, Blizzard left work on the dot of five that afternoon and got home in plenty of time to do the baby's bath time and read him a bedtime story, which improved his mood significantly. However, at one point, Michael laughed and the sound reminded Blizzard of the laughter of Janice Poulter's children the previous evening. The thought brought his mind back to Doris Hornsby and it was a pensive John Blizzard who put the baby to bed and went back down to the dining room. Fee had just served the pasta and they sat down at the table.

'I got the letter from HR today,' she said.

'Did it say what we expected?'

'Yes. They want a decision on my return to work within the next couple of weeks.'

It was the latest decision in a relationship which had started when they met after Fee, a policeman's daughter who was much younger than Blizzard, transferred to work as part of the Western Division CID team. She had lived with him for the best part of two years and the subject of her return to work had been occupying their thoughts more and more as the date approached.

'You any nearer to a decision?' asked Blizzard. He reached for his glass of red wine.

She shook her head.

'You?' she said.

'I can't pretend that the money won't come in handy but it's got to be your call. What does your gut instinct tell you?'

'That I love being with Mikey but that, whenever you tell me about your day, it reminds me how much I miss the job.'

'You wouldn't say that if you'd had a day like mine,' said Blizzard.

'No further forward?'

'No, and Arthur has warned me off Martin Hornsby. Says I've let it become a distraction.'

'He may be right.'

Blizzard gave her a rueful look.

'Maybe you *should* go back to work,' he said. 'At least I'll be able to tell you what to think then.'

'Like that's ever going to happen.' She raised her glass. 'Cheers.'

Chapter ten

Next morning, the briefing room at Abbey Road Police Station was packed as excited newspaper journalists, radio reporters and television crews waited to hear Blizzard provide an update on the murder investigation. As the room hummed with anticipation, the inspector sat behind a desk and eyed the journalists with little enthusiasm. His relationship with the media had always been difficult but he acknowledged that they could prove useful when it came to challenging cases. The inspector was also acutely aware that he was no closer to apprehending The Latch Man and hoped that the murder of Edith Bradley might loosen a few tongues. After providing some basic details, he threw open the event to questions.

'DCI Blizzard,' said a local newspaper reporter. 'You say that people living in the villages to the west of Hafton can be reassured that the police are doing everything to keep them safe, but surely you must acknowledge that the murder of Edith Bradley has caused them great consternation?'

Blizzard looked to the back of the room where Arthur Ronald was watching proceedings with trepidation; the superintendent knew from bitter experience the problems involved in bringing Blizzard and the media together but it was the line of questioning which they had expected and for which they had prepared.

'I do acknowledge that, Charles,' said Blizzard. 'That is why we have increased police patrols in the area and why our officers are working hard to bring the killer to justice.'

'Are you sure that The Latch Man is responsible for the murder?' asked another reporter. 'It seems a big jump from break-ins to murder.'

'It is difficult to be certain,' said Blizzard. He was selecting his words with care; there was a need to present a united front. 'However, that is the most likely scenario and is the one on which we are basing our inquiries.'

'But you are nowhere nearer to catching him?'

'Not as such, no.'

'Given his escalation from burglary to murder, are you not afraid that he may strike again?' asked another reporter.

'I am.' Blizzard looked directly into the lens of the nearest television camera. 'That is why this morning I am appealing directly to The Latch Man himself. If you are not responsible for the death of Edith Bradley, then you should contact me so that we can clear this matter up. If I do not hear from you, I have no alternative to believing that you killed her. It's your call.'

Another reporter stood up. Blizzard recognised him as a local freelance who contributed stories to one of the national tabloid newspapers. The two men had frequently clashed over what Blizzard viewed as his sensational reporting.

'DCI Blizzard?' asked the reporter. 'Is it true that you have been linking the death of Doris Hornsby with that of Edith Bradley?'

'Where did you hear that?'

'Well, there has been a lot of police activity at her home in Caitby Mallard. Is there a connection?'

'Only that Doris had also been burgled, which we are investigating as a matter of routine.'

'But I understand that you yourself have been there several times,' said the reporter. 'That does rather suggest that there may be more to it than meets the eye, does it not? Particularly given the somewhat colourful past of both women – if we can call it that.'

Blizzard glanced at Ronald again; the superintendent's expression suggested caution.

'Such speculation would be an unwelcome distraction,' said the inspector. He stood up and gathered his papers. 'And as you all know, I have never involved myself in speculation. Thank you, ladies and gentlemen, if you need anything else, talk to the press office.'

He stalked out of the briefing room where Ronald joined him in the corridor.

'Well played,' said the superintendent. 'The last thing we want is for them to dig up all that gangland stuff.'

'But if they can work it out…' said Blizzard darkly and headed off down the corridor.

Ronald frowned as he watched him go; the same thought had occurred to the superintendent.

Blizzard had been back in his office for less than ten minutes when Chris Ramsey walked into the room.

'Got a minute?' asked the detective inspector.

Blizzard motioned for him to take a seat.

'Why can't we put a name to The Latch Man, Chris?' he asked.

'Because he's a professional, guv. Leaves nothing behind. All neat and tidy.'

'Yes, he is, so are we really saying that a man like him would do what was done to Edith?'

'Maybe he panicked.'

'A man who bows when he is disturbed during a break-in does not panic. Anyway, we digress, what can I do for you?'

'The Dutch police have been on again. They reckon the guys who came through Hafton ferry terminal may be drug dealers.'

'What makes them say that?'

'They have talked to Interpol about the CCTV taken at Rotterdam before they drove onto the ferry and have decided that the driver looks like a guy called Geoff Hays.'

'The name doesn't ring a bell. Do we know him?'

'*We* don't but the Dutch do. They say he's a drug trafficker. Last time they heard of him, cocaine was his thing and they wonder if he and his pals have their eyes on opening up a new market in Hafton.'

'That's all we need. Some trigger-happy chancers muscling in on the local boys' turf. It can't end well.' Blizzard thought of the way that George Leys had been gunned down all those years previously. 'It never does.'

'They wonder if it's OK to send someone over to see us? Work together on it?'

'Sure.'

'I'll fix it up,' said Ramsey.

The rest of the day passed without further progress and by 6pm Blizzard felt in dire need of time to think, which is why he found himself walking across the wasteland on the edge of the city centre. It was hot and humid and Blizzard was seeking refuge in one of his boltholes, a ramshackle old railway engine shed. Police officers turned to all sorts of recreation to escape the pressures of the job: Colley was a rugby player, Ramsey was a martial arts exponent, Sarah Allatt a keen cyclist. For Blizzard, the son of a train driver, the escape was provided by the railway preservation society which he chaired and which used the shed close to the main station to restore steam locomotives. The contrast between the challenging nature of his job and the physical discipline of working with his hands had always helped him focus his thoughts.

He had just donned his overalls and reached down a spanner from the rack, intent on spending half an hour at work before heading home to Fee and the baby, when there was a grating sound as the door to the shed juddered reluctantly open. Blizzard scowled at the noise but the scowl disappeared when he saw that it was Colley.

'How's the chuff-chuff?' asked the sergeant. He eyed the rusted boiler dubiously. 'Looks like it's only good for scrap to me.'

'It's definitely not scrap. And for your information, it is not a chuff-chuff, it's a steam locomotive. One of the Gas Board ones. Used to run between the–'

'You should get out more. Or less.' He stepped over a pile of metal cables. 'Anyway, enough of playing trains. I came to tell you that your little plan worked. Control just received a call from The Latch Man – he wants to see you.'

Chapter eleven

'He's playing games,' said Blizzard.

It was approaching midnight and he and Colley were standing on the darkened platform of a long-dead railway station situated amid terraced streets close to the city centre. The only light was from their torches and the pale orange glow of the streetlamps that filtered through the gaping holes in the rotting timber roof, through which they could make out the occasional star glimpsed amongst the ragged clouds. Although it was the middle of the night, the temperature was still warm and muggy and the detectives were standing in shirtsleeves as they waited for The Latch Man.

The reason that Blizzard suspected him of playing games was the location. The inspector's passion for railways was well known – he had appeared in the local newspaper several times in relation to the preservation society's work – and it seemed clear that The Latch Man had chosen Garden Street station as their meeting place with a carefully judged sense of irony. Surveying the platform, which was stained with pigeon droppings, the deserted ticket booths and the darkened offices, just visible through doors that hung off rusting hinges, Blizzard felt a strong sense of history.

'This place deserves better,' he said.

'It deserves to be demolished,' said Colley. 'It's a bloody death-trap.'

'But stations like these are an important part of railway history, David. Think of all the things that Garden Street has seen.'

'Doesn't do it for me, I am afraid.' Colley glanced at his watch. 'Five minutes to go. Do you think he'll show?'

'Not sure. He's making all the rules.'

The answer came with the scrape of a shoe and the emergence of a figure from the shadows at the far end of the platform. The detectives could not make out his features in the semi-darkness but could see that he was tall and slim. Judging his age was difficult but he was not young, of that they were sure. Something about his angular silhouette suggested someone in his fifties, maybe his sixties. As he walked towards them, The Latch Man's movements were smooth, fluid, almost cat-like. He stopped thirty feet away and stood eying them for a moment, his features still tantalisingly obscured by the shadows.

'Are you The Latch Man?' asked Blizzard.

'Well I'm not here to catch a train.' The voice, which Blizzard thought had the faintest hint of a southern accent, possibly even London, was strong, calm, and assured. 'And this must be the doughty sergeant. Come to give you moral support.'

'That's me.' Colley lowered his voice so that only Blizzard could hear. 'We could rush him.'

'I suspect that by the time we got there, he would be long gone. Let's hear him out.' The inspector's next words were louder and addressed to The Latch Man. 'You are to be congratulated. You have given us a real run-around.'

'I like to oblige.'

'Why did you want to see us?' asked Blizzard.

'I saw your press conference on the news. I want you to know I did not kill Edith Bradley. I may burgle houses, Chief Inspector, but I do not kill.'

'Why should I believe that?'

'It's not my style. You know that.'

'But you could be lying. For all we know, you just want to take the heat off yourself.'

'*You* don't think I killed her,' said the man.

'Maybe not but I still need to get you under lock and key, though. Why don't you give yourself up – clear things up?'

'I am afraid that I have a natural aversion to cells.' The Latch Man gave a low chuckle. 'You don't leave the door open at night.'

'But unless we talk to you, we can't eliminate you from the murder inquiry.'

'You are talking to me now. Besides, I did not come to engage in a conversation. I have delivered my message and have nothing left to say.'

'So where do we go from here?' asked the inspector.

'Where we came from,' said The Latch Man. 'Me back into the shadows, you back to your railway engines. Besides, your two officers out there in the car must be getting bored. It is them in the unmarked Nissan, isn't it?'

'Yes, but–'

'Good night, gentlemen.'

The Latch Man turned on his heel and started to walk back down the platform.

'OK, get him, David,' hissed Blizzard.

Colley set off at a sprint but The Latch Man half-turned, spotted the movement and disappeared, without seeming to hurry, through one of the side doors. The detectives ran after him, Colley the first to career into the small office, which was shrouded in darkness.

'Where is he?' exclaimed the sergeant, flashing his torch around. 'He can't just have vanished into thin air!'

They heard a scraping noise, and, as their eyes grew accustomed to the gloom, saw a door in the corner of the office. Bursting into what had once been a storeroom, they saw a shadowy shape deftly remove a couple of wooden planks from across the window and dart out into the night.

Blizzard yelled into his radio.

'He's on the move, Chris! Coming out of the station now!'

Colley dived through the window, cursing as he crashed to the ground outside, grazing his shin on the gravel. Blizzard took a little more time and carefully eased himself through the jagged hole. As he jumped out and regained his balance, he could see that Ramsey and Allatt had leapt from the car and started to run across the wasteland, hurdling the old barrels and piles of bricks. Colley was ahead of them, closing rapidly on The Latch Man, who was fleeing towards the tall wire fence running along the nearby railway line.

'Got him,' breathed Blizzard.

For a moment, The Latch Man turned. It looked as if he was about to surrender but a rumbling sound attracted his attention and he gave a wave, ducked down and slipped through a hole in the fence. Seconds later, he had darted across the railway lines as a freight train approached. By the time the train had passed, The Latch Man had vanished.

'Damn,' gasped Blizzard. He was blowing hard as he thumped a fist against the wire. 'Damn, damn, damn!'

'This has been cut,' said Colley. He had crouched down and was examining the hole. 'He must have done it before he arrived. He's good, I'll give him that.'

Ramsey walked up to them.

'I've asked uniform to look for him,' he said. 'I had them on standby.'

'Somehow I do not think they will find him,' said Blizzard.

The inspector stared back over the wasteland in silence for a moment or two, noticing that the bedroom lights had started to come on in the nearby street as people peered out of their windows to see what was happening.

'Did you believe him?' asked Colley. 'Did someone else kill Edith Bradley?'

Blizzard, who was not as fit as the rugby-playing sergeant and was still struggling to catch his breath, considered the question for a few moments.

'Yes,' he said at last. 'I believe him.'

'If it helps,' said Colley. 'So do I.'

Chapter twelve

'Have you seen this?' asked Arthur Ronald as he walked into Blizzard's office the next morning. He dropped the tabloid newspaper onto the desk. 'Hardly going to make our life easier.'

'Unfortunately, I have,' said Blizzard. He looked at the front page which bore a picture of police cars parked outside Edith Bradley's cottage, accompanied by the headline *Gangland link to pensioner's death*. 'We could have done without it.'

'Certainly could. Martin Hornsby's lawyer has already been on to complain.' Ronald sat down at the desk. 'Like I told you, Doris's death has become a distraction.'

'Methinks Martin doth protest too much. Besides, I did try to steer the media away from the angle.'

'I know, I know.' Ronald sighed. 'I hear you lost The Latch Man last night.'

'We did, yes, but not before he had told us that he did not kill Edith Bradley.'

'And do you believe him?' asked Ronald.

'I do, yes.'

'So, what's the next step?'

Blizzard glanced up at the wall clock.

'Well, in five minutes,' he said, 'Chris is bringing the Dutch officer along for a briefing on our friends in the van.'

'Drugs, they think?'

'Apparently. It could make sense. We've had a few reports of more cocaine on the streets in recent months. Nothing major but if the Dutch cops are right, our friends are planning to change that.'

'Need to nip it in the bud and it'll do us good to be seen to be doing something.' Ronald looked at the newspaper again. 'Be nice to get some good headlines. Keep me informed, will you?'

He stood up and headed for the door, turning back as he reached the corridor.

'Oh, before I forget,' he said. 'HR are writing to Fee about her maternity leave.'

'She's got it already.'

'And is she thinking about coming back to work?'

'She's not sure yet.'

'Be good to have her back. She's a good officer. Although, I'm not sure the chief will want her back in Western CID. He's been tightening the rules up on couples working together.'

'She'll be happy wherever you send her.'

'I am sure she will,' said Ronald. He headed out into the corridor. 'After all, who'd want you as a boss?'

'Thanks for those kind words.'

'Don't mention it,' replied the superintendent's voice from the corridor.

Blizzard smiled but the smile was wiped from his face when he looked once more at the newspaper headline. There was a knock on the door and Chris Ramsey walked in, accompanied by a slim, dark-haired woman in her mid-thirties.

'Morning, guv,' said Ramsey. 'May I introduce Sergeant Sophie van Beek from Rotterdam?'

Blizzard stood up and shook her hand.

'Welcome to Hafton,' he said. The inspector motioned for her to take a seat. 'Chris looking after you, is he?'

'Yes, thank you,' said van Beek. She sat down at the desk. 'Although I'm not sure about his coffee.'

She opened her briefcase and produced a sheaf of papers.

'We've just been going through what the Rotterdam police have on our friends in the van,' said Ramsey, also sitting down. 'Trying to work out what connection they have with Hafton.'

'And what have you come up with?'

'Precious little, I am afraid,' said Ramsey.

* * *

PC Eddie Garbutt guided the patrol car into Louisa Street shortly after 10am and glanced at the constable sitting in the passenger seat.

'What number was it again?' asked Garbutt.

'Twenty-three,' said Jane Eeles. 'Half-way down on the right. The caller said people have been turning up at odd hours. Thinks the occupants may be dealing drugs.'

'But there's nothing on file?'

'No, if it is a drug house, it's a new one.'

As the car approached number twenty-three, the front door opened and a man emerged with his cap pulled down to obscure his features. When he saw the patrol car, he ducked back into the house.

'Now does that look dodgy or does that look dodgy?' said Garbutt, pulling the car into the kerb and switching the engine off.

* * *

'What we have,' said Ramsey, gesturing to the papers piled up on the desk, 'is pretty thin, if I'm honest. Fair comment, Sophie?'

Sophie van Beek nodded and pulled out several grainy printouts of images from CCTV cameras, which she spread out on the table for Blizzard to see. The inspector leaned over to examine them; he was enjoying the chance to consider something other than the controversy swirling around the murder of Edith Bradley. Having initially established his reputation as a drugs squad detective inspector in Western Division, investigating the trafficking of narcotics was something with which John Blizzard felt most comfortable.

'So, what am I looking at, Sophie?' he asked. He glanced up from the images.

She tapped a couple of pictures showing the vehicle travelling on a motorway.

'We believe that is the vehicle that ended up burnt-out on wasteland in your city,' she said. 'It was purchased in Antwerp a day after the incident with the gun. We suspect they thought Antwerp was far enough away for us not to make the connection. They were right, we only clocked them after they'd got through Rotterdam ferry terminal second time around.'

She held up the only image that offered a view of the driver.

'This was taken just before they drove onto the ferry,' she said. 'As you can see, it's not a particularly clear picture but one of our team believes that it's Geoff Hays.'

'God knows how you can be sure of that.' Blizzard looked unimpressed at the grainy image. 'Anyway, assuming that you're right, what do we know about him?'

'Not an awful lot. He's English and features in a number of intelligence reports linking him to drug trafficking but he's not big league, as far as we can ascertain, and we don't think he's been particularly active in recent years.'

'And we've never heard of him?' asked Blizzard. He looked at Ramsey.

'I am afraid not, guv. Whoever he is, he's not one of ours.'

'There were three of them, as I recall,' said Blizzard. 'Do we know who the others might be, Sophie?'

'The intelligence reports identify a number of known associates,' said van Beek. 'However, none of the names match those on the ferry company's passenger list so we think that they are travelling on fake passports. Without better CCTV images, we cannot be sure, and none of the names mean anything to DI Ramsey. We think that Hays was the one who threatened our guys with the gun but none of them have a history of using firearms previously so it's a bit of a mystery.'

'It certainly doesn't give us much to go on,' said Blizzard. 'I mean, we can't even say for definite that they are in the city, can we?'

* * *

Eddie Garbutt stopped the patrol car outside number twenty-three and he and Jane Eeles got out of the vehicle. As they approached the house, the front door swung open and the man in the cap appeared, brandishing a handgun at them.

Garbutt took a step forward.

'Drop it,' he said.

'Get back!' shouted the man.

'Don't do anything stupid,' said Garbutt. He held up his hands in a gesture of surrender.

The constable took another step forward and the man pulled the trigger. The bullet missed the officers and slammed into a parked car but, before they could react, he fired again and, this time, the bullet struck Garbutt in the shoulder, sending him crashing to his knees with blood spurting from a gaping wound.

The man loosed off a third shot as a terrified Jane Eeles dived for cover behind another parked vehicle. Again, he missed and the bullet struck a wheelie bin. Before he could fire again, three more men ran out of the house and, with the gunman still pointing his weapon at Eeles, they climbed into a car and sped down the street and out of sight amid the squeal of tyres.

Jane Eeles crouched next to the car for a few moments as she waited for her heart to stop pounding then reached with a shaking hand for her radio. Within minutes, the skies above Hafton were filled with the wailing of sirens.

Chapter thirteen

'So, we hit them and we hit them hard.'

John Blizzard stood at the front of the briefing room at Abbey Road Police Station later that morning and allowed his eyes to roam, settling for a second or two on each of the officers seated before him as he waited for his words to sink in. He could see from their faces that they had had the desired effect. Nothing got pulses racing more than feeling collars and the shooting of Eddie Garbutt had shocked everyone.

'I want to hear doors going in,' said Blizzard. He paced along the front of the room. 'I want to turn the tables on these scumbags.'

There was a ripple of applause round the room. Everyone loved a Blizzard Special.

'OK,' said the inspector. 'You have your targets and you know your teams. DI Ramsey is co-ordinating things, so if you want to say what a brilliantly-planned operation this is then talk to me, if you have any complaints about it, talk to him.'

There was some laughter and Ramsey grinned ruefully. Not a man blessed with a sense of humour, he had found himself growing used to the chief inspector's dry jokes after working with him for several years.

'The addresses you have been given,' said Blizzard, 'are all houses where we know drugs have been sold over the past six months. Most of them we have raided before.'

He glanced at Sophie van Beek, who was sitting on the second row.

'If our Dutch friends are right,' he said, 'that's what all this is about.'

Blizzard paused, eyes roaming round the room again for effect.

'And let's do it for Eddie Garbutt,' he said. 'Nothing will aid his recovery better than knowing that we have got the man who shot him.'

There was a murmur of appreciation and a hubbub of conversation and scraping chairs as the officers stood up and headed for the door.

'You,' said Colley, sidling up to the inspector, 'should be on the stage.'

'Thank you,' said Blizzard. He looked at the approaching Ramsey. 'OK, Chris?'

'Certainly am.' Ramsey shook his head in disbelief. 'Can't remember the last time I had this many officers available.'

Graham Ross walked up to them.

'Versace,' said Blizzard. 'Anything from the search of the house in Louisa Street?'

'Loads of prints,' said Ross. 'But no one we know.'

'And the guy who was with them had it away on his toes with the others,' said Ramsey. 'The car they used was torched on wasteland a couple of streets away. This lot are very careful.'

* * *

Late morning found Blizzard and Sophie van Beek standing in a Victorian terraced street, watching as a team of firearms officers prepared to raid one of the houses.

'Are you sure they're in there?' asked van Beek.

'Not really,' said Blizzard. 'But it's been used by drug dealers before, apparently.'

A firearms sergeant walked over to them.

'Happy for us to go in?' he asked.

'Yeah, sure,' said Blizzard. He gestured to the television crew standing nearby. 'And make it look good.'

Blizzard's dislike of the media did not blind him to the fact that they could be useful sometimes and this promised to be the kind of coverage you could not buy. In addition, he reasoned, positive media coverage would push the Edith Bradley case off the front pages and stop people asking awkward questions. Moments later, and with a tearing of timber and a cacophony of bellowed warnings, the officers smashed their way through the front door.

'Come on,' said Blizzard.

He and van Beek followed the team into the hallway where a couple of men in ragged T-shirts and scuffed jeans were being handcuffed by officers, amid much protestation. Blizzard walked up to one of them.

'What's your game?' asked the man.

'We are investigating the shooting in Louisa Street.'

'I know nowt about that,' said the man.

However, Blizzard sensed an uneasiness in the tone of voice.

'Sure?' asked the inspector.

'Yeah, sure.'

'Because if you do know anything about it, now would be the time to tell me.'

The man shook his head.

'I'm saying nothing,' he said.

Blizzard nodded at a nearby officer.

'Take him away,' he said.

'Do you think he *does* know something?' asked van Beek.

'I'm not sure. Nobody seems to know anything about Hays and his pals. Come on, let's get back.'

As they headed out into the street, a middle-aged woman approached them.

'DCI Blizzard?' she said.

'That's me.'

'I just wanted to say thank you on behalf of the people in the street,' she said. 'We've made several complaints about people coming to the house at all times of the day and night but nothing has happened.'

'Thank you,' said Blizzard. 'Although it should not take the shooting of a police officer to make us take action. I'll find out why you were ignored.'

'How is your officer?'

'He's in surgery but it looks like he'll be alright.'

Back at the police station, the reports came in steadily over the next few hours and, by the end of the day, eleven houses had been raided, thirteen dealers arrested, £15,000 worth of drugs recovered, £10,000 of cash located and three handguns seized. Shortly before 4pm, Blizzard was standing in the custody suite, watching the latest of the arrested men being brought in – a burly man who was cursing and hollering as Allatt twisted his arm behind his back and told him to be quiet. Colley walked over.

'She's shaping up nicely,' said the sergeant.

'She certainly is. Still no sign of our gunman?'

'Not yet, I am afraid. Mind, this little lot might loosen a few tongues.'

'Hopefully,' said Blizzard. 'At least it'll stop people asking about Edith Bradley.'

'Maybe not.' Colley held up a scrap of paper. 'This just came in. There's someone who wants to meet you.'

'Who?'

'Doris Hornsby's beloved Bill Gordon. Says he has a story to tell…'

Chapter fourteen

'I saw it on the news about your raids on the drugs houses,' said the old man. He nodded his approval. 'Very good. Very good, indeed.'

'Thank you, Bill,' said Blizzard. 'We've got thirteen in custody and several more released under investigation.'

'Under investigation? Modern jargon!' Bill Gordon shook his head. 'We did it differently when I started out. Forget files and reports, we would have taken them out the back and given them a good kicking. Oh, don't look like that. Don't tell me that there are not times when you would not happily do the same?'

Neither Blizzard nor Colley replied. It was early evening and they were sitting in the former detective chief inspector's small room at a residential home in the north of the city. On the wall hung three pictures, Bill at his daughter's graduation, him standing side by side with his son in a cricket team and a black and white picture of a much younger Bill Gordon receiving a commendation from his chief constable. The man himself was well into his eighties now. A thin man, he sat tall and proud in his armchair as he faced the detectives, who perched on the edge of the bed. His face was almost gaunt, the chin wispy with white stubble, but his eyes glinted with life.

Blizzard nodded at the picture showing the chief constable.

'What was the commendation for?' he asked.

'Locking up the guy who shot George Leys. You know about George, I take it?'

'Some. Not all.'

'He ran the criminal underworld in Hafton, did George. Started out with robberies then moved into the protection racket, intimidating pub and club owners and controlling the supply of black-market alcohol stolen from warehouses and lorries. It was big business.'

'What about George's sons?' asked Blizzard. He had always been fascinated by tales of the city's criminal past. 'How did they fit into it?'

'Martin was a bit of a fusspot. He had nothing to do with anything like that but Eric, now he was a nasty piece of work. I was not sad to hear that he died in that car crash. Him and Tony Bradley. I lost count of the times they left their victims smashed up in the gutter. They feared no one, not other villains, not us, no one.' He gave a slight smile. 'Except Doris. Everyone was frightened of her. George was not the sharpest pencil in the box and Doris was the brains behind everything.'

'Did you not arrest any of them?' asked Blizzard.

'Arrest, yes, get them into court, no, although it was not for want of trying. When I took over CID at Beggs Lane – before they put up those silly prefabs at Abbey Road – they told me my main job was to get George but he was always one step ahead of me. If you ask me' – Bill leaned forward conspiratorially – 'he had someone on the inside. I tried every trick in the book to get at the Leys family but nothing worked.'

'And yet Doris spoke very highly of you,' said Blizzard. There was a slight edge to his voice.

Gordon surveyed him through beady eyes, the change in tone not lost on him.

'I was not on the take, if that's what you are suggesting,' he said tartly. 'Doris liked me because I was a gentleman and, in return, they obeyed the rules: never backchat a police officer, never harm any of us, never target our families. Not like today with these dealers acting as if it's World War Three. I saw the television report on what happened in Louisa Street.'

'I apologise,' said Blizzard. He held up his hands. 'I was out of order.'

'Apology accepted. Mind, that's not to say that we didn't have bent officers, just like I'm sure you do. It's just that the villains knew how to play the game. Things are different now, I think.'

'They may have been the good old days but someone still shot George,' said Blizzard. 'What happened?'

'He and the boys had been drinking in The Elephant down Romby Street – you probably won't know it, it was demolished years ago when they built that filling station. Anyway, they were the last to leave, sometime around midnight it was – no-one dared call time on George Leys. As they walked onto the street, a car drove past and a shot was fired. George was dead before he hit the ground.' Bill Gordon shook his head. 'Senseless, absolutely senseless.'

'I heard it was some kind of turf war,' said Blizzard.

'It was. George and the boys had hooked up with some villains down in London. At some point, the lads from London got the idea that they could take over the operation.'

'But you got the shooter?' said Colley.

'Chap called Robinson. He holed up in a guest house over near the railway station and me and my sergeant went in and picked him up. Room eleven, Hayles Hotel, I'll never forget it.'

'Why?' asked Colley.

Gordon glanced up at the black and white photograph of himself receiving his commendation.

'Because his gun jammed,' he said.

There was silence for a few moments as he relived the scene, his eyes moist with the memory. Blizzard and Colley were silent, recalling their own experiences of danger down the years, putting themselves in Gordon's place.

'That's when I knew that things were changing,' said Gordon at length. 'George would never have tried to shoot a police officer.'

'And Robinson?' asked Colley. 'What happened to him?'

'Died in Hafton Prison. Got into a fight with some local lads and got himself stabbed.'

'Revenge?' asked Blizzard.

'Not organised if it was. After the shooting, it all fell apart. Doris could see that things were changing. Eric and Tony had fled to Spain and she went straight – married that funny little pawnbroker.'

'And the turf war?'

'We put ourselves about a bit and the Londoners didn't try again.' Gordon smiled. 'Like I said, gentlemen, the rules were different then.'

'Fascinating stuff,' said Blizzard. He glanced up at the wall clock. 'Why did you want to see us, Bill?'

'Well…' The old man's eyes gleamed. 'This might get you somewhere. See, if I was still in the job, I would reckon it was all a bit strange that Doris Hornsby had died so soon after Edith Bradley. Any officer worth his salt would think the same, right?'

Blizzard glanced at Colley but said nothing.

'Anyway,' said Gordon. His eyes glinted as he leaned forward in his chair. 'Guess who has just got a job working here?'

'Give us a clue,' said Blizzard.

'Annie Meadows.' Gordon sat back with a satisfied look on his face.

'The nurse who looked after Doris Hornsby?'

'Exactly. When I told her who I was, she asked me to pass on a message. Look closer at Martin Hornsby, she said.'

'Why?' asked Blizzard.

'That's up to her to tell and you to ask, Chief Inspector. She'll be back on duty at eight in the morning.'

'OK.' Blizzard stood up and shook the old man's hand. 'We'll come back. Thank you for the tip-off.'

'Want another one?' asked Gordon. 'About The Latch Man? First, can I ask, do you think that he killed Edith Bradley?'

'Well, I don't think it would be right–'

'Come on, I was a copper for the best part of forty years.'

'OK, no, I don't,' said Blizzard. He sat down on the bed again. 'It was different from the other break-ins. They were classier. Neater. No violence.'

'In which case, the only guy I know who could carry out burglaries that skilfully is Denny Buglass.'

'Who's he?'

'One of George's old pals. He was a master burglar, was Denny.' Gordon's voice betrayed admiration. 'We only got him by luck when a patrol spotted him early one morning after a job. Denny was known for being a gentleman – he would never have killed anyone. He was disturbed by one old dear but all he did was apologise and leave without taking anything.'

'I've never heard of him,' said Blizzard. He looked at Colley. 'Have you?'

'Nope.'

'I'm not surprised. He operated mainly on the east side of the city and I heard that he went straight when he came out. Bought a corner shop. Not sure where, somewhere in the city. Don't know if he still has it, it was the best part of twenty years ago. Might have retired.'

'Would he not be too old for burgling by now?' said Colley.

'You're never too old,' said Gordon, with a smile. 'At least that's what I keep telling some of the women in this place.'

The detectives smiled at the joke.

'It's worth a look, if nothing else,' said Blizzard. 'I don't suppose you know who fenced Denny's stuff?'

'There was a guy up here but he died not long after Denny was sent to prison – and, as I recall, some of the classier stuff, jewellery, that kind of thing, went to someone down in London. Denny never gave him up and we never found out who he was.'

'London, eh?' said Blizzard, recalling the encounter at Garden Street railway station. 'And what about…?'

Gordon gave a shake of the head.

'I am rather tired,' he said. 'Good evening to you, gentlemen.'

And he closed his eyes, the audience at an end. The detectives stood up, not sure what to do for a moment, then stepped out of the room.

'Interesting,' said Blizzard as they started to walk along the corridor.

'Is it really, though?' said Colley. 'I mean, it's a nice history lesson but that's about all. Isn't it just an old cop yarning on about the good old days?'

'But the London connection may be interesting.'

'I guess.'

The sergeant wrinkled his nose at the smell of stale urine in the air then shot his boss a sly look.

'This could be you in a few years,' he said.

'Yes, thank you, Sergeant.' Blizzard shuddered as he glanced through the open doors of the rooms with their blaring televisions and feeble old men and women slumped on their beds. 'When I get to that stage, you can shoot me.'

'What do you mean when?' said Colley.

Chapter fifteen

'I can't see anything in here to explain why they would pull a gun on police officers,' said Chris Ramsey.

The detective inspector dropped the Dutch police file onto Blizzard's desk and sat back in his chair. It was 7am the next morning and he and Sophie van Beek were sitting opposite Blizzard, mugs of tea in hand. Outside, the sun was breaking through the thin cloud and the temperature was starting to build again. Blizzard picked up the file and flicked through it.

'Are we even sure that it was this Hays fellow and his mates?' he asked. He dropped the file back onto the desk.

'As certain as we can be, sir,' said van Beek. 'All our inquiries suggest that his closest associates are a couple of Englishmen – Gerry Lawson and Brian Makepeace.'

'And what do we know about them?'

'Makepeace is the older of the two. Not sure how old he is, though. Lawson is in his thirties. The new CCTV images we have turned up suggest that they're the ones travelling with Hays. They certainly look similar to the descriptions we have, although that information is a few years old. It's all a bit lightweight, I am afraid.'

'It certainly is,' said Blizzard. He reached out and flicked onto another page. 'It says here that Makepeace and Hays were arrested ten years ago in Belgium on suspicion of drug trafficking but released without charge. They've not been arrested since?'

'Not that we can find,' said van Beek. 'And even then, it was only low-level stuff. Cocaine but not much of it. As you can see, we have more on Lawson but he's also been a low-level dealer. Three or four convictions in Spain, the last one eight years ago.'

'What do you make of it, Chris?' asked Blizzard. He dropped the file onto the desk and looked at his detective inspector.

'The names mean nothing to us, no one recognises the descriptions, there are no links with Hafton that we can find and they're only low-level drug dealers, when all's said and done. Why on earth would they keep pulling guns on police officers? That's what I don't understand.'

'And the fourth man who was with them? He's local, I presume, since he did not come in with the others?'

'Presumably, but we do not know who he is. Whoever the others are, they seem to be new boys in town. We'll keep looking but I'm not very optimistic.'

'So, what now?' asked Blizzard.

'Be happy with what we've got,' said Ramsey. 'The raids did us a lot of good. We nicked plenty of dealers and landed ourselves some good newspaper headlines into the bargain, which is always helpful for community reassurance. May stop us getting calls saying that we're not doing enough to stop drug dealing. But as for our gunmen, I have no idea.'

Blizzard looked at van Beek.

'And you?' he asked.

The Dutch officer shook her head.

'I'm hoping to get some more information today,' she said. 'But, as it stands, if we don't turn anything useful up, I'll head back.'

Blizzard stood up.

'Well, keep me informed,' he said. The inspector unhooked his jacket from the back of his chair and headed for the door. 'If anyone wants me, I'll be with Annie Meadows. Talking about another situation that doesn't make any sense.'

* * *

The inspector and Colley arrived at the elderly people's home shortly after 8am and, after showing their warrant cards to the receptionist, were ushered into a small office where an uneasy-looking Annie Meadows joined them a few minutes later.

'I didn't mean for you to come to see me,' she said, taking a seat. 'I've only just started working here and my new boss won't be impressed.'

'Refer him to me if he gives you a hard time,' said Blizzard. 'This is a murder inquiry, Annie, and you may have important information for us. Look closer at Martin Hornsby, you told Bill Gordon. What does that mean?'

The nurse did not reply.

'You can't just say something like that and leave it,' said Blizzard.

'But I don't want to be involved.'

'Newsflash, Annie, you *are* involved.'

'But Martin–'

'Forget Martin,' said Blizzard. 'I'll ask you again – why do you want us to look closer at him?'

'I wasn't totally honest when I talked to you last time. Doris *did* confide in me. She told me that Martin was in debt.'

'Now that is interesting,' said Blizzard. 'Do you know how he ran up the debts?'

'His investments had been doing badly and he was struggling to pay his bills.'

'Do you know how much he owed?' asked Colley.

'Doris did not know exactly. A lot. Thousands.'

'So, do we take it that he started looking at Doris's money?' asked Blizzard.

'He did, yes. Doris told me that, after Martin started seeing her more and more last year, she gave him money to clear off what he owed. She said she felt pressured into doing it. Then when I heard that she had changed her will in his favour, well, I started thinking.'

'Do you think she wanted to change it?'

'No, but I think that she was frightened of him,' said the nurse. 'You've met him, you know what he's like.'

'Yes, but I'm not sure that someone like that would frighten Doris Hornsby.'

'Maybe not the old Doris, Chief Inspector, but she was frail and she felt vulnerable. That's why she employed me, I think, to speak up on her behalf, but Martin made it clear that her private affairs were nothing to do with me.'

'Did he stop taking money from her after his debts had been paid off?' asked Colley.

'I don't think so. He had got a taste for it by then. Started spending money on holidays abroad, a new car, new clothes for Myra.' Annie shook her head. 'She's just as bad as he is. Horrible little woman.'

'Did not Doris challenge him about what was happening?' asked Blizzard.

'She tried to. There was a terrible row. He tried to get me to go but I stood my ground. After that, he never spoke to me again but he started distancing her from her friends and family. Doris was distraught when he told her that she could not see the grandchildren. People like Marion Rowbotham kept trying but, in the end, even they gave up. Edith Bradley tried to arrange afternoon tea a couple of times but Martin put an end to that as well.'

'How much did he take from her?' asked Colley.

'Doris said it was more than sixty thousand pounds.'

The sergeant gave a low whistle.

'And that wasn't enough for him?' he asked.

Annie Meadows shook her head and lowered her voice even though there was only three of them in the room.

'He just kept asking for more,' she said. 'Doris told me that there was another argument and that he had lifted his hand, like he was going to hit her. It was a side to him that she had never seen. She was shocked. *I* was shocked when I heard. I'd always thought him unpleasant but not violent.'

She paused, gathering her thoughts. The detectives stayed silent; the experience was clearly traumatic for the nurse.

'That was when she told me that she thought he had tried to kill her,' she said eventually.

'Kill her?' said Blizzard. 'Are you sure about that?'

'It was the week before she died. I was away visiting a friend and Martin agreed to come and administer her sleeping pill.' Annie's voice was so quiet now as to be barely audible. 'Doris didn't want him to do it. She'd said a couple of times that he'd try to do away with her, but I put it down to paranoia. She was becoming much more anxious. Anyway, Martin gave her the pill but twenty minutes later, she woke up to see him leaning over her, clutching a pillow in his hands. Martin said that he was puffing it up to make her more comfortable.'

'And do you think he was?' asked Blizzard.

'All I can say is that a few days afterwards, Doris was dead and I had been ordered never to come back to the cottage.'

'But the death certificate is pretty clear,' said Colley. 'It says that she died of natural–'

'It's not worth the paper it's printed on, Sergeant. I know the doctor, he's approaching seventy himself and hungover half the time. What's more, he's got a dozen villages in his area and most of his patients are elderly. If you ask me, he'd have taken one look at Doris and assumed that she was just another old dear dying of natural causes. Who wouldn't?'

'I wish you'd told us this earlier,' said Blizzard.

'I thought about it but what would you have said? Doris was a confused and frail old lady who was increasingly agitated. Anyone looking at her could see that she was not long for this world. You'd have laughed at me.'

'Actually,' said Blizzard, glancing at Colley, 'I don't think we would.'

Twenty minutes later, he and Colley were walking across the car park to the inspector's vehicle.

'You said there was something iffy about it,' said the sergeant.

'I did indeed.'

'So, what happens now?'

'Now,' said Blizzard, unlocking the car, 'I think it's time for the dead to rise from the grave!'

Chapter sixteen

'I'm sorry, John, I'm still not convinced,' said Arthur Ronald. He looked at Blizzard, who was sitting at the other side of the superintendent's desk cradling a mug of tea. 'You're going to need more than a bit of tittle-tattle before you dig the old girl up.'

'Come, on, we've got more than that,' said the inspector. 'We've got motive, means and opportunity. What more do you need?'

'OK, maybe you have but it's all circumstantial, isn't it? You need an awful lot more to justify the exhumation of Doris Hornsby, sunshine. And just as the media are starting to forget about the gangland links to Edith Bradley, this would put it back on the front pages, wouldn't it?'

'Yes, but–'

'I really can't see the chief sanctioning this, John. He's hacked off enough about that front page as it is.'

'Focus on Edith Bradley, you said. Well, I have and I think her death may be connected in some way with what happened to Doris Hornsby. I can't understand why you won't listen to me.'

Silence settled on the room as they looked at each other unhappily. It was 5pm and they had debated the issues endlessly for the best part of a day, the two old friends trying to put aside personal affection to discuss the matter with professional detachment but nevertheless at times finding themselves in sharp disagreement. Those around them observed that it was like watching a married couple bickering.

'All I am saying is that there's something that warrants further investigation,' said Blizzard. He reached for the top sheet of a pile of papers that he had placed on the desk. 'Last time I checked, that was why you employ me. The neighbours are convinced of it, too.'

'Yes, well I hope that none of them has told Martin Hornsby what you are thinking. That lawyer will have us all up in the High Court at this rate.'

'They're sworn to secrecy.'

'You know neighbours, John. Gossip-mongers, the lot of them.'

'Maybe so but we needed their help. Martin and Myra are very private people and some of the neighbours have had suspicions about his mother's death ever since they heard about it. Marion Rowbotham certainly did.'

'I keep telling you that we need more than that.'

'Well, for a start we've got more on his money problems now.' Blizzard looked down at the sheet of paper on the desk. 'Sarah Allatt has been doing a lot of digging. Annie Meadows was absolutely right, although she only knew the half of it. Turns out that he borrowed money to make a series of investments just before the big crash of 2008. Then the stock market collapsed and he was left deeply in debt.'

'How deep?' Despite his reservations, Arthur Ronald found himself intrigued.

'Looks like he borrowed £100,000 from various banks but fell behind on the repayments.' Blizzard flicked onto the next sheet of paper. 'According to this, he owes at least

£150,000 and one of the banks has been looking to repossess his house. Doris was the answer to his prayers, Arthur.'

'Let me have a look at that,' said Ronald.

The superintendent scanned the page then looked at his friend.

'OK,' he said, 'I agree it *could* be seen as motive. But lots of people fall into debt without resorting to murdering their mothers and you still can't prove anything, can you?'

'I told you what the nurse said. The man tried to kill Doris.'

'Yes, but can you really rely on the word of a woman who has good reason to cause trouble for the man who sacked her – and who only got it from an old dear who was probably suffering from dementia anyway?'

'That's why I want to exhume her. Why are you so opposed to this, Arthur?'

'Because exhumation is just about as serious as it gets and if you get it wrong, it brings down all sorts of trouble on our heads. And also because we cannot get away from the fact that the death certificate says that she died of natural causes.'

* * *

Doctor Richard Brewis sat in his consulting room and looked across the table at the grim-faced detectives. Even from where David Colley and Sarah Allatt were sitting, they could smell the stale stench of last night's alcohol on the GP's breath.

'I am sorry you have struggled to get hold of me,' said the doctor. 'I've been away for a couple of days. Recharging the batteries. Amazing how all those sick people can be bad for the health.'

He gave a little smile and tried to sound relaxed but the detectives sensed unease in his voice. And his eyes told a story of anxiety.

'You wanted to talk about Doris,' he said when neither officer replied. 'Can I ask why?'

'Because we're not happy with the death certificate you signed,' said Colley. He held up the document. 'Leaves a few questions that need answering.'

'Questions?' The doctor gave them what he assumed to be a reassuring smile but which merely served to increase the sense of a worried man. 'Surely, it was all very straightforward.'

'We're not sure it was,' said Colley.

'Look, Sergeant, Doris Hornsby was a very frail old woman with a range of health problems, not least of which was a bad heart. She'd had poor circulation for years and death could have come at any time really. It's a wonder she got this far.'

'I'm sure that's right. Nevertheless, we do have concerns. Can I ask if you examined the body?'

'I did, yes.'

'Did you check for injuries?'

'Injuries?' The GP looked at him in amazement. 'Why on earth would I check for injuries?'

'So, there weren't any injuries?'

'I'm sure there weren't, no.'

Colley gave him a hard look.

'*Did* you examine the body, Doctor Brewis?' he said. 'I mean, really examine it?'

'Well, I suppose you could say that it was a somewhat cursory examination,' said the GP reluctantly.

'How cursory?' asked Allatt. 'Is there a chance you could have missed something? The odd bruise?'

'I suppose it's possible.' The GP sighed. 'Look, you're right, I didn't examine her that closely but I was happy that she died of a heart attack. There may have been the odd bruise but so what? Old people have got lots of them. They're always falling over or bumping into things.'

'Are you this lackadaisical with all your patients?' asked Allatt.

'Now look here, young lady. For your information, I had eleven house calls that day alone and I certified seven deaths that week, all very frail old people. I can't be expected to…'

His voice tailed off as Colley stood up.

'Thank you, Doctor,' he said. 'We may be in touch again.'

Once the detectives were in the car park, Colley took his mobile out of his jacket pocket and scrolled down his contact list. Back in Arthur Ronald's office, Blizzard listened to the sergeant for a few moments, ended the call and looked at Ronald.

'I suspect you'll have to agree with me now,' he said. 'Front page headlines or not…'

Chapter seventeen

'You want to do what!' exclaimed Martin Hornsby. He leapt to his feet, sending the chair flying backwards, and strode angrily over to the office window, where he slammed a fist into the sill.

'I want to exhume your mother's body,' said Blizzard. 'And will you sit down! This is difficult enough without you bouncing about like a bloody jackrabbit.'

'Difficult for whom, Chief Inspector?' said Hornsby. He glared at the detective. 'You're just a bloody troublemaker.'

It was the day after Ronald had decided to back Blizzard's request and the atmosphere in the inspector's office had been thick with tension from the moment that Martin Hornsby walked into the room. His mood at being summoned was not improved when he saw Janice and Robert already sitting there. Hornsby had turned furiously on his heel and made as if to go. Only a curt command from Blizzard had persuaded him to turn back and sit down next to his niece and nephew. He did not look at them.

Now, Hornsby stood at the window and looked balefully at Blizzard, his right fist bunching and un-bunching repeatedly, the knuckles glowing white. Janice and Robert were equally horrified at what they were hearing, the former's face ashen and strained, tears starting in her eyes, the latter's unable to conceal the shocking impact of the chief inspector's revelation.

'Sit,' said Blizzard again. He gestured to the chair, his voice softening a touch. 'Please, Mr Hornsby, you are only making things worse.'

Hornsby hesitated for a moment then nodded dumbly. Blizzard waited for him to settle back into the chair and noticed again how he still did not even glance at his niece and nephew. As all three sat dumbfound, the irony of the situation struck the chief inspector forcibly – that for a brief second or two, and for the first time in decades, they were united, if only in their shock and grief.

'Now that you have calmed down,' said Blizzard, 'let me say something before I explain why I wish to exhume Doris. You are here, Martin, because you are next of kin. I invited Janice and Robert as a courtesy to your brother's children, a courtesy which you seem not to have granted to them over the years. It is time that this silliness between you came to an end. Eric Leys is long dead and this feud should have died with him. It's time for a reconciliation.'

'Bloody social worker now, are you?' said Hornsby with a sneer.

'I do not think your attitude is helping proceedings,' said Blizzard. He was well used to the antipathy of those he encountered in his job; he often told Colley that the most difficult ones to interview were those who remained calm and kept things civil. Those who ranted and raved just brought out the worst in Blizzard – or the best, depending on which way you viewed things.

'You had better have a good reason for this!' said Hornsby. He had become agitated again. 'Because this is an outrage. I'll have you dragged over every damned coal in Hafton for this! I have some pretty important friends in this city–'

'I am quivering in my boots at the prospect of being approached by senior figures in the accountancy profession,' said Blizzard. He allowed himself a slight smile.

'This is no time for jokes,' said Hornsby, glaring at him again.

'Indeed, it's not,' said Blizzard. 'If I am wrong, you will have every reason to voice your distaste at what has been done but if I am right, there will be a lot of questions to be asked... and I think that you can give us the answers.'

Martin chewed his lip furiously but said nothing.

'Does this mean that you think Granny was murdered?' asked Janice. She turned pained eyes on Blizzard.

'All I can say is that we would not have taken this step unless we had good reason.'

'Absolute lunacy!' exclaimed Hornsby. 'The death certificate said it was natural causes.'

'Yes, well, we remain to be convinced. We have information that means that we need to have her body examined again.'

'What information?'

'I am not at liberty to divulge that yet.'

'Well, I refuse to let it happen!' said Hornsby. 'It is preposterous and I will be protesting in the strongest possible terms!'

'Protest all you like, Martin, but you can do nothing to stop it. We have all the permissions in place.' Blizzard adopted a business-like tone. 'Now, under the rules of exhumation, it must be done at midnight and we have agreed with the vicar at Caitby Mallard Church that it will take place tomorrow night. I am offering you the chance to be present.'

'An outrage!' snapped Hornsby again. 'I shall be talking to my solicitor. This will only go ahead over my dead body...'

'Or your mother's,' murmured Blizzard so low that Hornsby could not hear.

'What did you say?'

'Nothing,' said the chief inspector.

Hornsby glared at him again.

'Well, if you think it is necessary,' said Janice, 'I think you should go ahead with it. What do you think, Rob?'

Her brother, who had not uttered a word throughout the entire meeting, shrugged.

'Whatever,' he said. 'They seem to have made their minds up, anyway.'

'OK, Inspector,' said Janice. 'You will get no objections from this side of the family.'

'Thank you,' said Blizzard. It was sincerely meant.

'Well, you will get plenty from me!' exclaimed Hornsby. He stood up and stalked to the door, turning to jab a finger at Blizzard and fire a last bitter comment. 'You have not heard the last of this. I will fight it all the way and when I win, I will have you writing bloody parking tickets until the day you die.'

Blizzard waited until he had gone then turned to Janice and Robert.

'I am sorry about this,' he said. 'Truly I am. I know how difficult this must be for you.'

'Granny's passing and the ill-feeling that has surrounded it has been very hard for us,' said Janice. Her voice quivered with emotion. 'I just want it to be all over. Can you tell us anything?'

'Not really, except to say that your grandmother was extremely frightened of Martin.'

'Frightened?' Janice looked surprised. 'Granny? She was never frightened of anyone.'

'I know this is difficult to take but, by the end, your grandmother was a very scared little old lady.'

Janice started to cry. Robert put an arm round her and looked at the chief inspector.

'I always thought that he was a bastard,' he said.

'It certainly looks like he has some questions to answer,' said Blizzard. 'Anyway, I would appreciate it if you could keep this to yourselves. I don't want it to be the subject of parish pump gossip in the village.'

Five minutes later, brother and sister were gone, escorted out of the police station's back door by Colley so as to avoid the raging Martin. Blizzard stood at the office window and looked out at the car park where he saw them get into Robert's vehicle and edge their way out on to the main road, Janice dabbing her tear-filled eyes with a tissue. The chief inspector noted that the blue skies had gone and that the dark clouds were starting to gather again. Another storm on the way. Sometimes, he reflected gloomily, his office could be the loneliest place in the world. As his dark thoughts crowded in on him, there was a knock on the open office door and in walked Sarah Allatt.

'Guv,' she said, 'I've got something that will really interest you.'

'I hope it's good news,' grunted Blizzard. He returned to his desk and gestured for her to take a seat. 'I could do with some. What have you got?'

'You asked me to find out if there is anything to link Doris Hornsby or Edith Bradley to London,' said the detective constable. She sat down.

'And?'

'And I tracked down one of the people in Scawby that I had not talked to before – she has been on holiday and only heard about Edith's death when she got back last night. She noticed a strange car in the area a couple of times before she went away. The second time it was near Edith Bradley's house. Fortunately, she's part of Neighbourhood Watch and she kept a record of the number plate. It came from London.'

'Did it now?' Blizzard leaned forward in his chair. 'Did you check for the owner?'

'He's a bloke called Paul de Montfort.'

'Very posh,' said Blizzard.

'Sounds it, yes. He's an antiques dealer in Bayswater, specialising in antique jewellery. Just like the type being taken by The Latch Man.'

'And Bill Gordon said that our friend Denny had a London fence in his heyday, did he not? This gets better and better, Constable. How old is this De Montfort fellow, do we know?'

'Not sure exactly. The Met say mid to late sixties.'

'About the same age as Denny Buglass. It's certainly possible that there is a link. The old gang getting back together, perhaps. He got a record, this De Montfort fellow?'

'According to the Met, he was suspected of handling stolen goods but it was a long time ago and he was never prosecuted. The DS I talked to reckons that he is legit now. His shop is very upmarket. A lot of wealthy customers. Hugh Grant bought something there, apparently. She has never heard of Denny Buglass. Neither had any of her team.'

'No reason why they should, Sarah. They've probably got no idea that Hafton even exists. This is all very interesting. Excellent work.'

'Thank you, guv.' She beamed at the compliment; John Blizzard had always been a hard man to please. 'What do you think we should do next?'

'What do *you* think we should do?'

'I think we should pick De Montfort up.'

'Yes, so do I,' said Blizzard. 'Ask the Met if they'll do it for us, will you? Maybe get someone to run him up here?'

Allatt had only just left the room when Chris Ramsey walked in.

'We've got another possible sighting of our gunmen,' said the detective inspector.

'Another false alarm?'

'Who knows? It's from a woman in Raglan Street who read about it in the paper and thought she recognised one of the descriptions as someone she's seen at the house next door to hers.'

Blizzard stood up and reached for his jacket.

'Better call out the cavalry then,' he said.

'They're already on the way, guv.'

'Sophie gone back to Holland?'

'Yeah, couple of hours ago.' Ramsey followed Blizzard out of the office. 'I'll let her know if this comes to anything but don't hold your breath. Oh, and we've got another update on Eddie Garbutt.'

'How is he?' asked Blizzard.

They started walking along the corridor.

'Much better,' said Ramsey. 'They reckon he'll be out in a week or so. Could be six months before he's back at work, mind. His shoulder is pretty badly mangled.'

* * *

Fifteen minutes later, they were standing at the end of a terraced street on the edge of the city centre, watching as armed units moved into position and uniformed officers created barriers to keep bystanders back. The air was filled with the clatter of rotor blades as the force helicopter hovered above. Colley ambled up, wearing a Kevlar vest.

'This could bugger up tonight,' he said to Blizzard.

'Yeah, it may well do. Hope not, though, we've booked the babysitter. It's the first night out we've had in ages.' Blizzard glanced at his watch. 'What time did we say we'd be at yours?'

'Half seven.'

'What's the occasion?' asked Ramsey.

'Wedding anniversary,' said Colley. 'I've missed the last two and Jay'll kill me if I miss this one.'

'I wouldn't worry,' said Ramsey as the armed officers completed their preparations. 'If it's anything like the others, it'll be a waste of time.'

Blizzard looked along the street.

'Do we know if anyone is in?' he asked.

'Doesn't look like it.'

A uniformed officer walked over to them.

'How do you want to play it?' she asked Blizzard.

Blizzard noticed a television van arrive. He knew that there'd be more.

'Let's go in now,' he said. 'I don't want another media circus. Too many false alarms and it'll look like we don't know what we're doing.'

Within a minute, armed officers had forced their way through the front door, yelling warnings as they went. Two minutes later, an officer reappeared and shook his head. Blizzard and Ramsey walked down the street and entered the house to be greeted by a musty smell. They walked slowly from room to room, each one laden with the stench of damp.

'Not sure anyone's been here for a while,' said Blizzard as they walked back into the hallway.

'The neighbour must have been mistaken,' said Ramsey. 'She *is* eighty-six and doesn't see that well.'

'Now you tell me,' said Blizzard. 'Come on, let's get out of here. I've had enough of crumblies for one day.'

Ramsey chuckled as the detectives walked back into the street. Blizzard watched the armed officers head back to their vehicles.

'So where are they, Chris?' he asked.

'Well away from Hafton, if they've got any sense,' said Ramsey.

Blizzard shook his head. The alarm bells were still ringing in his brain.

'No,' he said. 'I think they're still here. Something important brought them to Hafton – and they're prepared to take some big risks to achieve what they're after.'

Chapter eighteen

'But will it not feel strange?' asked Jay. 'Me and Dave talked about it. Raising the dead would give me the collywobbles.'

'Not me,' said Blizzard. He lifted the glass of red wine to the light, swilled it round for a second or two, took a sip and gave an appreciative nod. He looked at Colley. 'We've done one or two of them and we've been alright, haven't we?'

'We have, yes, but Jay's right, they do feel strange,' said the sergeant. 'Unnatural.'

It was 9.30pm that evening and they were sitting in the terraced house which Colley shared with his wife, a willowy redhead in her early thirties. It was she who had suggested that Blizzard and Fee go round for dinner. 'You have to take the opportunities when they're there,' she had told her husband. Jay sometimes found Colley's irregular working life frustrating – her job as a primary school teacher tended to offer more regular hours – but she had always acknowledged that there would be times when he was late home. Over recent months, the sergeant had been keeping regular hours but in the days since the murder of Edith Bradley, she had seen less and less of him so when it looked like both men would be clear, she had suggested the wedding anniversary dinner.

After eating, the four of them settled down in the living room with its pastel shades and rustic prints and soft light afforded by a couple of table lamps and the flickering fake coal fire. Mellow jazz music was playing quietly in the background. Blizzard was in an armchair, glass of wine in hand, Colley was in another with a pint of bitter in a Hafton Rugby Club beer mug and the women were on the sofa with their wine.

'So, what *will* you feel?' asked Jay curiously. She looked first at Blizzard then at her husband. 'I mean, when the spades go in, what will you be thinking?'

'It's part of the job, I suppose,' said Blizzard. 'Not sure I think anything.'

'Yeah, and if it turns out she wasn't murdered, we'll just shove the old coffin-dodger back in her hole.' Colley caught sight of Blizzard's expression. 'What?'

'Can't you teach him how to use the English language?' the inspector asked Jay.

'He can't,' said Jay. She shot Colley an affectionate glance. 'He's a rugby player, remember.'

Then she was serious again.

'But–' She paused, struggling to frame the words. 'Exhumation can't be right, can it?'

'Meaning?' Blizzard looked at her intently.

'Well–' She paused again. 'I am not religious – I am not sure Dave would let me in the house if I was–'

'Too right,' said the sergeant.

'But, nevertheless, there is still a sanctity about death, isn't there? I mean, when you are put in the ground that is where you should stay. It's the way of things and digging someone up disturbs that balance. I don't know… I just think it's wrong, I guess.'

'But why should it matter?' asked Blizzard. He took another sip of his wine. 'When you're dead, you're dead. I mean, when I die, you can do what you want with me. See if I care.'

The inspector looked at Fee.

'Isn't that right, love?'

'I suppose so,' said Fee. 'But I'm with Jay on this one. It *does* feel odd.'

'I guess for me it would be more of a concern if I was religious,' said Blizzard. 'But I'm not. My mother was. She'd have disapproved of exhumation. Each to their own, I suppose.'

'What does the vicar think?' asked Jay.

'He'd rather it all went away. But it needs to be done. If Doris was murdered, we need to find out.'

Silence settled on the room as they sipped at their drinks.

'Your maternity leave must be coming to an end,' said Jay eventually, seeking to change the subject and looking at Fee. 'You had the letter yet?'

'Yes, just got it.'

'Do you know what you're going to do?'

Fee shook her head.

'Not yet. I quite fancy going back to work but things would be different.' She looked at Blizzard. 'I couldn't work with John, for starters. The chief constable's tightened up the rules since I went off to have Mikey.'

'And what do you think?' asked Jay, looking at Blizzard. 'Do you think she should go back to work?'

'It has to be Fee's decision,' said the inspector. 'But there's a lot to think about. Childcare, for a start.'

'We found a brilliant childminder when I went back after having Laura,' said Jay. 'I can let you have her number, if you like.'

Fee nodded.

'Please,' she said.

Blizzard picked up the bottle of wine and offered to top up Jay's glass, but she put her hand across it. Fee accepted when he offered.

'It's John's turn to get up with the baby if he wakes,' she explained.

'You sure, Jay?' said Blizzard, still holding the bottle.

'Yes, sure. I have already had too much. I learned a long time ago never to teach with a hangover.'

'We've been talking to a teacher over the past few days,' said Colley. 'I keep meaning to mention her, see if you know her. Marion Rowbotham. She's retired now. A somewhat formidable woman.'

'She sure is.' Jay chuckled. 'A character and a half.'

'You know her?' said Blizzard.

'Everyone knows Marion Rowbotham. She was the head at Moss Street Primary School. It was in a terrible mess when she arrived, but she turned it around – she really did. She was really cut up when the council closed it to make way for that new supermarket. Now, *that* was criminal. I think that's why she retired. Why were you talking to her?'

'She's a neighbour of Doris Hornsby,' said Blizzard. 'Got on very well with her, apparently.'

'Well she would do. They had plenty in common.'

'Why do you say that?'

'Marion Rowbotham's father was a villain as well,' said Jay.

'What?' exclaimed Blizzard.

'Don't you detectives find anything out?' she asked. She passed her glass over to Blizzard. 'Coming to think of it, I will have a top-up, John. I've just remembered that they've got PE with Mr Ranson first thing. Funny chap, he–'

'Forget Mr Ranson's peccadillos,' said Blizzard. He poured the wine. 'Tell us about Marion's father.'

'Someone told me that he used to work for George Leys.'

'Really?' Blizzard was sitting up now, listening keenly. 'What did he do?'

'Drove getaway cars, I heard. He was sent to prison for it. Came out and started his own second-hand car business.

Did very well, in fact. I did hear that he was the one who bought the house in Caitby Mallard for Marion. She'd never have been able to afford it on her own.'

'Now that is interesting,' said Blizzard. He held up his wine glass. 'Cheers, everybody.'

Chapter nineteen

Next morning saw the emergence of Denny Buglass. Ever since Bill Gordon had suggested his name in connection with The Latch Man inquiry, detectives had been trying to track him down – if only to satisfy themselves that he had nothing to do with their investigation. Easier said than done because no one seemed to know where he was until one of the East Side detectives achieved the breakthrough purely by chance. While working an unrelated case, he strolled into a scruffy back street newsagents to buy a chocolate bar and was served by a tall man with curly brown hair greying slightly at the temples and a frame that hinted, despite a slight paunch, at more athletic days. Something about him sparked the officer's curiosity and, wandering back into the street, he glanced up at the nameplate above the shop. *D. Buglass and Son.* He had found their man.

So it was that within an hour Blizzard and Colley strolled into the shop and eyed with interest the man behind the counter. Buglass greeted them with a friendly smile.

'Can I help you?' he asked.

'I am not sure,' said Blizzard. He noted immediately that the voice had the flat Hafton accent and sounded nothing like that used by the man in the railway station. 'Bill Gordon suggested we talk to you.'

'Bill Gordon,' said Buglass. 'That old rogue.'

'Yes, he talks fondly about you as well.'

'So, do I assume that you are police?' Buglass sounded more guarded this time. 'You've got the look.'

The detectives held up their warrant cards so that Buglass could read them.

'So, I guess it was your officer who came in this morning?' said Buglass. 'I thought he was a copper. I can spot you a mile off. How can I help you, gentlemen?'

'We are conducting inquiries into The Latch Man,' said Blizzard.

Buglass stared at them for a moment then roared with laughter. The detectives watched him in bemusement.

'Pray, what is so funny?' asked Colley.

'Don't tell me that Bill Gordon fingered me as The Latch Man?' chuckled Buglass. 'He always did have a vivid imagination, did old Bill, especially when it came to writing statements, if you know what I mean.'

'He said you were the only one with the skill to do what The Latch Man does,' replied Blizzard.

'Maybe once.' Buglass looked over to the door as a middle-aged woman entered the shop. 'Er, do excuse me, gentlemen. Talk of crime does not go down well with the punters. Now then, Mrs Pallister, what can I do for you, my dear?'

When the woman had gone, clutching her pint of milk and twenty Regal, Buglass chuckled again.

'I am afraid I will have to disappoint you,' he said. 'I mean, look at me, I'm sixty-seven with a bad back. I have all on to get out of bed in the morning some days, let alone break into anyone else's house.'

'How did you do your back in?' asked Colley.

'A fall in prison. It's not been too bad for the past few years but I slipped on ice last year and it's been murder ever since.'

'An unfortunate turn of phrase,' said Blizzard. 'Can anyone verify this bad back of yours?'

'I ain't a liar,' protested the shopkeeper.

'I'm sure you're an absolute saint,' said Blizzard. 'But that does not answer the question. Can anyone verify your bad back?'

'Check with my doctor if you want.'

'Oh, we will,' said Blizzard.

'I can't see the point of this,' said Buglass. 'My burgling days are a long time over.'

'But you did know George Leys, didn't you?' said Colley. 'And Doris Hornsby, for that matter. And Tony Bradley and his mother, I am guessing.'

'I have not made a secret of my criminal past. And I once met John Lennon at John F. Kennedy Airport but it doesn't mean I went round and screwed his house afterwards.' He gave them a slight smile. 'It would have been *A Hard Day's Night* in the cells if I had.'

Colley allowed himself a smile at the quip. There was something likeable about Denny Buglass. Blizzard did not seem to share the feeling and eyed the shopkeeper dubiously.

'Look, gentlemen.' Suddenly Buglass was serious. 'You can check my alibis if you want but there is no way I am The Latch Man. I served my time and hated every minute of it. When I came out, I resolved to go straight, and that is what I have done. I have a nice little earner here and, when I retire in a year or two, I will pass it on to my son. There is no way I would jeopardise all this by going back to the old ways. Even if I could.'

A man emerged from the office behind the counter. A squat, meaty character with bovine features, a snub nose and sunken eyes, he was wearing scuffed jeans and a tattered purple jumper. He looked at them suspiciously.

His demeanour reminded Blizzard of Robert Leys' surly expression.

'These men are detectives,' said Buglass. 'Gentlemen, this is my son Raymond.'

There was no answer from the man.

'Can you get those boxes from out the back?' said Denny to his son. 'We're running short of lager.'

Raymond disappeared back into the office. They could hear a door opening and a scraping sound as he started to move the boxes in the yard. Buglass turned back to the detectives.

'Have to rely on the boy for everything,' he said. 'My back, see.'

'So you keep telling us,' said Blizzard.

'Look, gentlemen.' For the first time, the façade slipped and his irritation showed through. 'I admit that in my time I was a burglar and a damned good one at that – never made a secret of that – but I served my time and I have no intention of going back to prison. I am sorry but I really am not your man.'

The façade returned and he smiled brightly and gestured to the chocolate bars ranged across the front of the counter.

'Snickers anyone?' he said.

A couple of minutes later, the detectives were back in the street and walking to Blizzard's car.

'If he has got a bad back, there's no way he's still burgling houses,' said Colley. 'I mean, look at you. You're useless when your back flares up.'

'Nevertheless,' said Blizzard. He unlocked the car.

'You surely don't still fancy him?'

'Not sure.'

'But what about the accent?' said the sergeant. 'There's no way that's London.'

'Assuming that we were talking to the real Latch Man at the railway station. Find out what you can about him, will you?'

'Sure, but we're wasting our time, guv. I told you, Denny Buglass is part of history.'

* * *

It took Colley several hours to unearth the information but by mid-afternoon, he was sitting in the inspector's office, his notebook open on his knee.

'I've been doing a bit of ringing round on the East Side,' said the sergeant as Blizzard handed him a mug of tea and returned to his seat behind the desk. 'And I reckon we might be onto something, after all.'

'Like I keep saying, a prophet in–'

'Not so quick, guv. It's not Denny, rather his bovine son. No, I reckon Denny's on the level. There's no way that he could have killed Edith Bradley. Bill Gordon was right. He's not the type to hurt anyone.'

'We sure?'

'Pretty much. A few weeks before Denny was arrested, he was disturbed by an elderly woman just after he had got into her house. He was edging his way up the stairs when she crossed the landing in her nightgown on her way to get a glass of water. She made as if to scream but Denny held a finger to his lips, said that she would not be harmed and left the house empty-handed. He even got her the glass of water before departing.'

'Does it not make him the kind of man who might bow to Doris Hornsby, though?' asked Blizzard. 'If we assume that the break-ins were committed by different people, that could still put him in the frame as The Latch Man, could it not?'

'Except for his bad back.'

'That's genuine then?'

'Happened when he was in Hafton Prison. Doing a seven-year stretch. It was never fully explained but it was believed to be the result of an assault, probably by his cellmate. I tracked down his GP, who confirmed it.' Colley took a sip of tea then glanced down at his pocketbook.

'Disc trouble. He was released from prison early on medical grounds. Had a couple of operations.'

'And he did not go back to his old ways?'

'Seems not. He bought one shop then another, sold them both, then got the one where we saw him today – he only purchased it a few months ago, which is why it took so long to find him. He's straight alright.'

'But not so Raymond?'

'No, he's a very different story.' Colley ran a finger down another page in his pocketbook. 'While his father was in prison, he and his mother went to live with her sister in Leeds and he started to run with the wrong people – theft, drugs, breaking into cars, then burgling a couple of old people's bungalows. He was in and out of prison.'

'Very interesting.' There was a gleam in Blizzard's eyes.

'It gets better. He's got a real temper on him, has Raymond. Got himself into a few punch-ups in pubs. Red mist stuff. If you are right and the burglaries were done by different people, he could fit the bill. He may not have the skills to be The Latch Man but he may have enough of a temper to attack Edith Bradley.'

'Except he's been in Leeds.'

'Not for the past year, he hasn't. His dad became so worried about him that he offered him a job. They live in the flat above the shop. He's still into the drugs scene, low level mainly. And the icing on the cake is that I sent Sarah back to the villages to see if anyone knew him and it turns out that he spent some time as a jobbing gardener, mowing lawns and doing weeding for the elderly residents. Among the places he worked were Caitby Mallard and Scawby and among his clients was none other than Edith Bradley.'

Blizzard sat forward.

'Really?' he said.

'Yeah. What's more, she sacked him for accidentally cutting down a prize rose bush. He also did some work for

Doris Hornsby but Martin fired him. Said it was a waste of money.'

'How come none of the villagers mentioned this?' asked Blizzard.

'No one made the connection. Raymond has not been seen in the area for the best part of a year. You want him brought in?'

'No, not yet.'

'But if we search his home–'

'*If* he is involved, he'll have got rid of anything incriminating the moment we left this morning. No, I want him watched.'

Not sure quite what to make of it all, the inspector left the office just after five, promising to see Colley for the midnight exhumation, and went for a walk along the river. This was another of the places he went when he needed to clear his thoughts and straighten his mind out and he strolled along the sandy foreshore for the best part of an hour, occasionally pausing to shy stones across the deep silt-brown waters, the late afternoon sun glinting off their surface. He also spent long minutes staring out at the chemical works on the other side. He was not sure why, but the works always had a calming effect on him, and as the water eddied and weaved its way down to the sea, and the waves lapped gently against the foreshore, things began to crystallise in John Blizzard's mind.

Chapter twenty

Caitby Mallard churchyard at midnight was an eerie place. The sense of foreboding among those who had gathered for the exhumation had been increased by the fog that had rolled in off the River Haft during the previous hour, shrouding the fields around the village and slowly snaking its way through the roads and lanes, wrapping itself round the houses and descending noiselessly to cloak the church.

Following a briefing at Abbey Road Police Station, Blizzard and Colley had set off shortly after 11.15pm. Driving through the deadened silence, unable to see the surrounding countryside, they lapsed into silence, each alone with their own thoughts as the enormity of what they were about to do began to strike home. Although neither was religious, Jay's comments the night before had illustrated the way that digging up the dead still touched deep nerves. For people who dealt with death on a regular basis, there was nevertheless something spiritual, sacred, about life, and something almost primeval about the process of exhumation. Despite their bravado of the night before, both officers felt uneasy at the prospect.

When the detectives arrived at the church, a small knot of people was standing at the front gate, held back by a couple of uniformed officers. Blizzard got out of the car and scanned them quickly, noting without much surprise that they included Marion Rowbotham. She gave a little wave. Blizzard said nothing but gave her a slight nod and pushed his way through the gate.

'She gets everywhere,' he murmured as he and Colley walked up the path.

'Who does?' asked the sergeant.

'That Rowbotham woman.'

'She's just being a good neighbour.'

'Possibly.'

Blizzard looked for Martin Hornsby among the group of people gathered in front of the church but he was not there. He had continued his efforts to have the exhumation called off until well into the evening but all his threats and those of his lawyer had come to nothing and Blizzard was relieved that he was not present; this was going to be difficult enough as it was.

Martin Hornsby's absence did not mean that the family was not represented at the graveyard and the chief inspector saw that Janice and Robert had both arrived. Janice, face pale and lined with the strain, was dressed in a long black overcoat, fastened to the top to keep out the clammy chill of the night, and a dark hat. She looked like she was attending a funeral, mused Blizzard, rather than an exhumation. Having said that, the inspector was not quite sure what one did wear to an exhumation. For his part, he was still wearing his suit and a dark windcheater. Robert had not taken much effort about his appearance and was dressed in a scruffy black anorak and tattered jeans. He had the usual surly expression on his face and did not acknowledge the officers' presence as they walked up the path. It was left to Janice to extend a hand. When Blizzard took it, he noticed that she was cold and clammy and that the hand was shaking slightly.

'I will try to make this as painless as possible,' he said.

'Thank you, Mr Blizzard,' she said. 'I didn't really want to come but Robert said we must. For Granny's sake.'

'I appreciate that you did. There should be someone from the family at a time like this.'

'So, is Martin not coming?' asked Janice.

'It seems not. Look, I really do hope this will not be too difficult for you but it is something we must do.'

'If it has to be done, it has to be done.' Janice glanced towards the gathering of neighbours at the gate. 'Can Marion be here?'

'Well, I'm not–'

'It would make me feel better. She's been very good to us, hasn't she, Rob?'

'She has, yeah.'

'How did she know this was happening?' asked Blizzard. 'Did you tell her?'

'Marion knows everything that happens in the villages,' said Janice. 'Can she come?'

'I suppose so.' Blizzard shouted down to the uniformed officers. 'Send Marion Rowbotham up, will you?'

The officers opened the gate and the pensioner walked up towards them and gave Janice a hug. There were a number of other people present outside the church, among them Arthur Ronald and the vicar of Caitby Mallard. For the clergyman, the past few days had been extremely trying as he found himself thrown into the centre of a situation beyond his experience. Like many involved, he felt that the dead were meant to stay in the ground and he was earnestly outlining his views on the subject to the superintendent when John Blizzard walked up.

'Ah, Chief Inspector,' said Ronald, relieved to have found a way out of the vicar's diatribe.

'Evening, sir,' said Blizzard. He extended a hand towards the vicar. 'Thank you for this, Reverend.'

'I must confess that it is most irregular,' replied the vicar. 'And I do not like it at all. As I was just explaining to your superintendent here, I specialise in putting them in the ground, not bringing them back. This is rather like the tale of Lazarus, I suppose.'

'Except one would hope that Doris Hornsby is not alive,' said Blizzard. 'Even I would have to sign up to your religion if she was, Reverend.'

The vicar looked uneasily at him, not sure whether the comment was meant seriously or whether it was a dark joke. Ronald looked at the reverend's confusion and allowed himself a thin smile. Colley ambled up.

'All ready, guv,' he said.

Blizzard glanced at his watch.

'Five to midnight,' he said and looked round the gathering. 'OK, ladies and gentlemen, shall we?'

Once they were away from the reassuring glow of the streetlights and in among the headstones, the atmosphere grew more tense. As they walked beneath the clawing fingers of the trees through long grass glistening with the light rain that had fallen earlier in the evening, with their path illuminated by flickering torchlight, shapes seemed to loom from the shadows, dancing and darting in the swirling mist. Behind them, the parish church loomed large and dim and silent.

The vicar, who was nervously leading the way, stopped at a shiny black marble gravestone, incongruous among the weathered and crumbling older ones that surrounded it. One of his predecessors had tried to persuade Doris Hornsby to select something more suitable but she had refused. The current incumbent pointed to the names Alf Hornsby and Doris Hornsby and the inscription *Together in His arms. May they rest in peace.*

'Sorry, guys,' murmured Blizzard, so low that no one else could catch the words. 'No rest just yet.'

He turned to the gravediggers.

'Here,' he said.

His words seemed to echo and to have no place in an oppressive silence. Blizzard hesitated for a moment then the church clock chimed twelve, the peals muffled in the fog.

'OK, boys,' he said.

The first spade went in and the small knot of people watched in reverential silence as the men worked. After a few minutes, there was the dull thud of metal on wood and the coffin was revealed. Heaving and panting, the gravediggers brought it to the surface. Everyone stared at it for a few seconds, even the hardened police officers moved by the moment.

'Well, there she is,' said Blizzard at length.

Janice stood arm in arm with Robert, sobbing gently.

'Oh, Granny,' she said softly.

Marion gave her another hug.

'Are you OK, love?' she asked.

Janice nodded.

'May I say a prayer?' asked the vicar.

'Of course,' said Blizzard.

As the reverend stepped forward and uttered a few halting words. Blizzard walked over to join Ronald, who was standing beneath one of the trees.

'I just hope we're right,' said the superintendent in a low voice.

'Bit late for that,' replied Blizzard.

The vicar finished and the coffin was carried carefully across the graveyard towards the waiting hearse. Slowly and silently, the small gathering followed the body back to the front gate where two figures loomed out of the misty orange glow cast by the streetlights. One was Sarah Allatt, the other a male detective.

'Who are they?' asked Robert suspiciously.

'A couple of our officers,' said Blizzard. He waited for everyone else to walk past before he spoke to the two detectives.

'Can't a man enjoy a quiet exhumation without being disturbed?' he asked.

'Sorry, guv,' said Allatt. Her eyes gleamed. 'But we've just arrested The Latch Man!'

Blizzard glanced at the coffin, which was being loaded into the hearse.

'Now you tell me,' he said.

Chapter twenty-one

What made it all the more difficult for Blizzard was that, on the face of it, Sarah Allatt and Detective Constable Gary Romanes had indeed caught The Latch Man, and very possibly the killer of Edith Bradley – if you believed that they were the same person. However, as Blizzard sat in the Abbey Road squad room after he had returned from the exhumation and listened to the detectives' story, his doubts kept growing. And doubts quickly turned to conviction.

The incident had happened after Raymond Buglass, dressed in black and carrying a haversack over his shoulder, sneaked out of the flat above the newsagents and clambered into his ageing Ford Escort. He edged the vehicle out into the street, clearly nervous because he glanced up and down the road three times before setting off. The detectives followed him in an unmarked vehicle with a mounting sense of excitement. Their sense of anticipation grew as they followed him out into the countryside and into the village of Hedgby, four miles from Caitby Mallard.

Once there, Buglass left his car at the entrance to one of the more attractive streets and crept towards the end house, an ivy-covered cottage nestling behind a low wall. Allatt and Romanes followed him on foot, crouching low as they watched him force the front window. They could clearly hear the sound of tearing timber as he prised it open with a screwdriver. As he began to climb in, the officers rushed forward. With a terrified squeal, Buglass span round and lashed out, catching Allatt on the side of the head with the screwdriver, sending her flying, but Romanes wrestled him to the ground. Allatt climbed unsteadily to her feet, blood dribbling from a gash to her cheek, and helped the constable subdue the struggling burglar. It was all over in a matter of seconds. Lights went on in nearby houses and the officers were able to ascertain from neighbours that the cottage belonged to an eighty-six-year-old widower who was away visiting relatives.

'So,' said Allatt, as the officers sat with Blizzard in the squad room at Abbey Road, 'what do you think? Surely, it's him?'

Blizzard did not reply immediately. He was acutely aware that such occasions were not the time to lose his sense of perspective; he had seen too many innocent men jailed because detectives leapt to wrong assumptions. What made it more difficult was the fact that everyone else had already made up their mind. It was 2am and word had gone round the police station that Allatt and Romanes had arrested The Latch Man. The adrenaline rush provided by their colleagues' admiring looks, generous comments and slaps on the back was enough to banish their fatigue after a long night. Romanes, the more seasoned of the two officers, was enjoying his moment in the limelight and Allatt was revelling in the excitement of her first major arrest. This was why she wanted to be a detective. This was what it was about.

Blizzard sighed as he surveyed their bright faces and wished he was somewhere else.

'Excellent work,' he said at length. 'But he is not The Latch Man.'

The faces fell.

'What do you mean it's not him?' asked Romanes. 'We caught him bang to rights, guv. If we hadn't nicked him, he would have screwed the old fellow's place.'

'No doubt about it,' said Blizzard. 'And that is why it was a good arrest but no way is he The Latch Man.'

'But–' began Allatt.

'But nothing,' said Blizzard firmly.

He turned round as a beaming Arthur Ronald walked into the room, followed by a more pensive Colley, in whom Blizzard had already confided his doubts on the journey back from the exhumation.

'Good result,' said Ronald happily. He nodded approvingly at Romanes and Allatt, whose face was still streaked with dried blood.

'The gaffer doesn't think so,' said Romanes.

Ronald turned enquiring eyes on his friend.

'It is a good result,' said Blizzard. 'And believe me, no one would like it to be him more than me, but it isn't. I am sorry.'

'Oh, come on,' protested Ronald. 'You can't keep throwing a dampener on things. Raymond Buglass fits all the criteria, a burglar preying on elderly women in the villages and with a history of violence. What's more, he's got a dad who probably taught him all the tricks of the trade. What more do you need?'

Blizzard looked at the crestfallen Romanes and Allatt then at the hopeful expression on Ronald's face and sighed again.

'Look,' he said. 'I am not throwing a dampener on anything. These two have done excellent work and the arrest of Raymond Buglass is a cracking result. I have already said that. I just cannot see him being The Latch Man – and as for Denny Buglass teaching him the tricks of the trade, give me a break. Prison damn near killed the man, do you really think he wants to go back? The guy has been straight for years.'

'Yes, but that does not mean Raymond is not The Latch Man, does it?' said Allatt. There was defiance in her voice. 'You'd have to have a pretty good reason to say that, guv, and I don't think you have.'

Colley, who had settled himself down in the corner of the room, feet up on a desk, sat forward slightly and held his breath; everyone knew that very few junior officers – and not that many senior ones – could get away with challenging Blizzard like that. Romanes' expression, formerly frustration, had now turned to one of unease at the tone of the constable's voice and Arthur Ronald said nothing, although his body language suggested he feared an explosion of anger from the chief inspector. Surprisingly, it did not come.

'Did you examine the window at the cottage?' asked Blizzard calmly.

'Yes,' said Allatt. She was thrown by the question and too busy worrying that she had overstepped the mark.

'Did you see anything?'

'Well, it was a bit of a mess but–'

'What kind of a mess?'

'Well, he had dug up quite a bit of the windowsill.'

'Exactly.' Blizzard turned to Colley. 'David, you examined Edith Bradley's home after her murder, I think? We both did.'

'We did,' said the sergeant. He lowered his feet to the ground.

'Was there any sign of what Constable Allatt here would call a mess?'

'No,' said Colley. 'No, it was a clean break-in, guv. Sweet as a nut.'

'And Versace and his forensics boys and girls – what do they say about The Latch Man?'

'That he leaves nothing.'

'Doesn't gouge out whole chunks of windowsill then?'

'No.'

'Exactly.' Blizzard turned to look at the others and this time it was his turn to have a touch of frustration in his voice. 'Do you not see? The Latch Man is a pro. A touch of class. Calm. Cool. Collected. He's highly skilled. Forensics hate him because he leaves nothing for them to work on. But that's not the case with Raymond Buglass, is it? He's a druggie who will do anything to get money for his next fix. The Latch Man would not be seen dead ripping out half a bloody windowsill to get in.'

Allatt and Romanes looked at the ground, disappointed but realising that what he said made sense.

'He's right,' said Ronald. He nodded reluctantly. 'Damn his hide.'

'Go and interview our Raymond,' said Blizzard gently to the two detectives. 'See what he says.'

Chapter twenty-two

Raymond Buglass sat and viewed the detectives across the interview room desk through sunken eyes. Everything about his demeanour suggested defeat but as they took their seats, the officers sensed something more, something deeper – fear. They could smell it in the oppressive atmosphere of the room.

'I can't go back to prison,' said Buglass before either of them could speak.

'You shouldn't go round burgling houses then,' said Romanes. He had not given up on his hope that they had caught The Latch Man. It did not last long.

'I don't,' said Buglass. 'It's the first one I've done for years.'

'Come on, Raymond, you'll have to do better than that,' said Romanes.

'It's true! I haven't done a burglary since I screwed a tobacconist in Leeds ten years ago.'

'So why do this one?' asked Allatt.

'I'm desperate for money.' Buglass sighed. 'I borrowed some cash for drugs from a moneylender. Jackie Rowlands. Operates out of The Red Lion behind the railway station.'

'We know him well,' said Romanes.

'Then you know what he's like. He's been leaning on me and I'm not the only one at The Red Lion either. He cut one of my mates a couple of weeks ago. He needed his bottom lip stitching back on so I weren't going to take no risks.' Buglass looked anxious. 'But don't tell Jackie what I said. He'll have me.'

'No promises,' said Romanes. 'So, the old guy whose house you broke into? Why him?'

'I knew that he kept cash in his bedside drawer and that he's gone away for a few days.'

'And how do you know that?'

'A mate of mine down The Red Lion told me.'

'And this mate of yours knew about the old man's money how, exactly?' asked Romanes.

'His mum cleans for the old feller. She'd mentioned the money before, then my mate overheard her on the phone about him going away. We were going to split the cash fifty-fifty.'

Romanes said nothing; it all sounded horribly plausible.

'Weren't you worried that you'd be caught?' asked Allatt. 'I mean, we have stepped up patrols in the villages since the death of Edith Bradley.'

'Yeah, but you can't be everywhere, can you? Besides, I'm more scared of Jackie Rowlands than I am of you.' Alarm flickered across his face. 'And you'd better not be trying to pin her death on me. I had nothing to do with that.'

'But you and her do have history, don't you?' said Allatt.

'It was only over some stupid roses – and it was ages ago. Like I'd kill the silly old bag for that.'

'And where were you when she was killed?' asked Romanes. It felt like his last shot at proving Blizzard wrong.

'The Red Lion. I'm there most nights, you can ask anyone.'

Half an hour later, with his statement written and signed, the interview was at an end and the detectives stood up and made as if to go.

'What happens now?' asked Buglass.

'You'll be kept in overnight and charged with burglary in the morning,' said Romanes.

'At least Jackie Rowlands won't be able to get to me.' Buglass gave them a half-smile. 'Every cloud, eh?'

Romanes nodded gloomily.

'One more thing,' he said. 'Did your father know what you were going to do tonight?'

'Na. I waited for him to go to sleep. He'd have only tried to stop me. He's straight is my dad.'

Romanes sighed and, while he took the prisoner to be locked up for the night, Sarah Allatt returned to the CID room with a heavy heart, fearful about what her previous outburst had cost her professionally. Blizzard was the only person in the room.

'How'd it go?' he asked.

'He admitted the burglary,' she said.

'Not sure he could do much else. What'd he say?'

'That he needed the money to pay back Jackie Rowlands. He knows him from The Red Lion. He's not the only one, apparently.'

'If I owed Jackie Rowlands money, I think I'd turn to burglary,' said Blizzard. 'We've been after him for years. Too many frightened witnesses. Every time we think we're getting close, they clam up. When you're back in tomorrow, I want you and Gary to check out what's been happening at the Lion but keep it low key for the moment.'

Allatt was silent for a few moments.

'I'm sorry,' she mumbled eventually. She felt the tears welling up. 'Have I ruined my career in CID?'

'Why would you think that?'

'Questioning your judgement.'

'The day you stop asking questions is the day that you stop being a police officer,' said Blizzard. 'It is still a damned good collar, and one that will reassure a lot of the people living in the villages. There is a lot of fear out there and the news that we have nicked a burglar will do wonders. That has to be a good result in anyone's book. You should be proud of yourselves.'

The glum look on her face suggested that his words had done little to make her feel better.

'Oh, come on,' said the chief inspector. 'He may not be The Latch Man but scumbags like Raymond Buglass need to be taken off the street. And think about it for a minute. What if the old chap had been at home and disturbed him? Who's to say that we would not have had another Edith Bradley on our hands? Eh?'

He fixed her with a quizzical look and she nodded.

'Now,' said Blizzard as Colley walked into the room, followed by Romanes. 'Do we know a friendly pub landlord who might still be serving at this hour to let these good people have a celebratory snifter for nicking Raymond Buglass? Preferably not The Red Lion.'

Colley glanced at his watch. It read 3.10am.

'You know, guv,' he said. 'I don't think that we do.'

'I reckon,' said Blizzard with a sad shake of the head, 'that in Bill Gordon's day, he would as sure as hell have found one. Things were different then, you know.'

Chapter twenty-three

Despite Blizzard's conviction that there was something amiss with the death of Doris Hornsby, the inspector still entertained lingering doubts as he hesitated at the door to the mortuary at the General Hospital later that morning. Colley, standing behind him, allowed himself a slight smile; the encounters between his boss and Home Office pathologist Peter Reynolds were legendary, fuelled by years of ill-feeling between the two men, and the sergeant was always asked for every last detail by colleagues at Abbey Road after they had taken place.

'You not going in?' asked the sergeant as Blizzard continued to hesitate, his hand resting on the door handle.

'Yeah.' Blizzard turned to look at Colley with a troubled expression on his face. 'But what if I'm wrong, David? What if I've been blind to the simple truth that Doris Hornsby was an old dear whose time had come?'

'It's a bit late to entertain thoughts like that. Mind, you'll be sorted for lunch for a few weeks, if you *are* wrong.'

'What do you mean?'

'Well, you'll not be short of humble pie, will you? Very good with ketchup, I'm told.'

Blizzard gave him a rueful look.

'I guess,' he said and led the way into the room.

Any doubts the inspector may have entertained were swept away by the pathologist's first words as he looked up from his examination of Doris Hornsby's body.

'Who on earth examined this one?' he said with a disapproving sniff.

'Her GP,' said Blizzard. 'I'm not sure that he was very thorough, mind. Said she was very ill and that she died of natural causes, didn't he, Dave?'

'That's right.'

'Well, he was a bloody amateur,' said Reynolds. 'These people should leave it to the experts. I have always said that.'

Blizzard did not reply. It was shortly after 10am and having had very little sleep following the exhumation, not helped by the baby waking up when he got in, he was not in the mood for Peter Reynolds. Not that he ever was. The detective even disliked him more than some villains. You knew where you were with a villain, he often said, but you just did not know where you were with Reynolds most of the time. He found the pathologist and his approach to the job difficult to understand.

Reynolds, who was now humming cheerfully as he continued his examination, made no secret of the fact that he had little time for people when they were living but found them fascinating when they were dead, regarding their bodies almost like works of art, whatever their state. Reynolds loved post-mortems and he was loving this one even more than usual. He knew that Blizzard disliked him and that stories of their encounters were eagerly seized up at Abbey Road Police Station. The pathologist always attempted to live up to expectations.

'You've found something, I take it?' asked Blizzard.

Something in the tone of voice made Reynolds look up again and he noticed Blizzard's anxiety. It was not something he was used to seeing in the chief inspector.

'Do I take it from your eagerness,' asked Reynolds, the faintest hint of a mocking smile in his voice, 'that you are worried that you might have overstepped the bounds on this one?'

'Just get on with it.'

Reynolds looked over to where Colley was leaning against the wall, enjoying the two men's meeting as usual.

'He doesn't get any better, does he?' said Reynolds.

Colley grinned and shook his head. Reynolds returned his attention to Blizzard.

'There's a lot riding on this, I think, Chief Inspector,' said the pathologist. He probed the body again. 'I hear this has been somewhat, how shall we say, contentious? After all, digging up old dears is hardly standard police practice, is it?'

'If Doris Hornsby died peacefully in her sleep, the chief constable will have my knackers for book-ends.'

'Well,' said Reynolds. He straightened up. 'Your chief constable will have to find a couple of those rather nasty little ceramic poodles, or something similarly tacky, to keep his books in order. From what I hear, they would rather suit the man. Like I said, Chief Inspector, the GP was an amateur.'

'What have you found?'

'Something very interesting,' said Reynolds. He walked over to the sink, washed his hands and dried them on a towel. He made sure that every action was slow and drawn out so as to increase the inspector's impatience. Eventually, he reached across to a drawer and pulled out an X-ray, which he held up to the light. 'I had these taken earlier. What do you see?'

'Quit the games,' said Blizzard curtly.

'Oh, please, do humour me,' said Reynolds, 'I do so like it when I can pull detectives' gonads out of the fire – or at least off the bookshelf.'

Blizzard glared at him.

'Shall we try again?' asked Reynolds. He held up the X-ray. 'What do you see?'

Blizzard looked at it and shrugged.

'Well, what I see,' said Reynolds, 'is that two of the neck vertebrae are cracked. Look closer.'

The chief inspector did so and this time could just make out, very faintly, very faintly indeed, the hairline cracks. Easy to miss but once you saw them, they were obvious and Reynold's trained gaze had identified them straightaway.

'What does it mean?' asked Blizzard.

'It means that someone exerted pressure on the old dear's neck,' said the pathologist. He replaced the X-ray in the drawer.

'Could it be an old injury?'

'What, from her rugby-playing days?' said Reynolds. He winked at Colley, who could not resist a smile.

'Will you answer the bloody question!' exclaimed Blizzard, his mood not improved by the interplay between the two men. 'Could it have been an old injury?'

'Had she complained of neck pain?'

'Not that we know of.'

'Then it's not an old injury. Besides, it looks recent, to me. I doubt she would have been able to go long without needing some form of medical treatment. No, I think it is a fair assumption that this was done shortly before death.'

'Or at the time of death?'

'Very possibly,' said the pathologist. 'There's also evidence of petechial haemorrhaging. I'm surprised that no one picked it up. The undertaker, if not the doctor.'

'The GP had signed the death off as OK, so they'd have had no reason to query it,' said Colley. 'How was the injury caused?'

'Well, if I was a betting man,' said Reynolds, 'and I am not – a particularly vulgar habit if you ask me – I would say that the fractures were caused by someone smothering her.'

'With what?' asked the chief inspector, the excitement clear in his voice.

'I don't know,' shrugged the pathologist. 'Could be anything. A pillow, something like that. She was a frail old bird, a hand might have been enough. Certainly, whoever did it would not have had to exert much pressure.'

'Got you,' breathed Blizzard. He headed rapidly for the door. 'Got you, you bastard.'

'I take it that is what you wanted to hear?' said the pathologist, watching him go. 'Don't feel you have to thank me.'

The inspector gave a deep sigh and turned to face him at the door.

'I am most grateful to you,' he said. The words stuck in his craw but he tried to make them sound sincere. 'Thank you.'

'Glad to oblige, Chief Inspector. Perhaps we in the medical profession are of some use, after all.'

'Don't push your luck,' growled Blizzard and left the room.

Reynolds winked at Colley again.

'You got enough?' asked the pathologist.

'Oh, aye.' The sergeant headed for the door. 'Plenty. The crack about her playing rugby was particularly good.'

'I do try to help, Sergeant.'

'And don't think it's not appreciated.'

When Colley had gone, the pathologist gave a chuckle and started humming as he returned to Doris Hornsby's body.

'I do love my job,' he murmured.

Chapter twenty-four

John Blizzard was besieged from all sides when he arrived back at Abbey Road Police Station from the hospital and walked into the CID room shortly after 11am, a cheerful expression on his face. There was a scraping of chairs as Allatt, Romanes and Ramsey all stood up at the same time and headed for him, talking at once. Blizzard held up a hand in protest.

'One at a time,' he said. He turned first to Romanes. 'Gary?'

'There's someone to see you,' said the detective constable. 'He's in your office. Dave asked him to come in.'

Blizzard looked at Colley.

'Who is it?' he asked.

'The guy from the Fraud Squad that I mentioned,' said the sergeant. 'He's an old mate of mine. Must mean that he's turned something up. I warned you about fiddling your expenses.'

'Yes, thank you for those kind words, Sergeant,' said Blizzard. 'You'll enjoy your next secondment. I hear being a traffic warden is a very satisfying job. OK, I'll see him in a minute. Next? Sarah.'

'I've just had a call from the Met,' said Allatt. 'They've checked De Montfort and all his usual haunts. Nothing.'

Blizzard pursed his lips.

'Pity,' he said. Tracking down the owner of the London-registered car spotted near the villages to the west of Hafton had become a top priority for the team. Even though they could not trace the car back to De Montfort, the revelation that he had a record for handling stolen goods had made him of great interest. 'We need to find out where he fits into the picture pretty damn quick. Where are we with Raymond Buglass?'

'We think we'll have to charge him with last night's burglary and that's all,' said Romanes. He still sounded disappointed. 'Forensics say that there is absolutely nothing to link him with the break-ins at the homes of Doris Hornsby or Edith Bradley and he's got alibis for both nights.'

'Says who?' asked Blizzard. He perched on the end of one of the desks.

'His dad vouched for the first one,' said Romanes. 'Swears blind that his son was tucked up in bed the night Doris Hornsby's house was screwed. Remembers it because they'd been watching a film together.'

'And Edith Bradley?'

'Raymond reckons he was down The Red Lion and the landlord has confirmed it. Apparently, he goes on benders at least once a week and is not capable of anything when he does. The landlord remembers that night clearly. Not sure he's a fan of Raymond Buglass.'

'But can anyone confirm the landlord's version?' asked Blizzard. 'I wouldn't trust him as far as I can throw him.'

'Nor me,' said Romanes. 'But the barmaid confirmed it. Raymond tried it on with her, apparently. Dead end, I am afraid, guv.'

'Not quite,' said Blizzard. He gave them a self-satisfied look. 'See, you need to be much less trusting of what people tell you. What did I tell you, Sarah, the day you stop asking questions is the day you stop being a police officer?'

'Guv?' said Allatt.

'Tell them,' said Blizzard. He looked at Colley, who had sat down at his desk by the window.

'The governor still wasn't convinced about Denny Buglass,' said Colley. 'Something did not feel right, did it?'

Blizzard shook his head.

'We were taking too much on trust,' he said.

'So,' said Colley, 'I contacted my mate who used to work in CID on the East Side but who is now with social security. He asked around and one of his colleagues remembered Denny Buglass.'

'What did he say?' asked Romanes. He tried to control the sick feeling that he and Allatt had missed something important.

'Well,' continued Colley, 'when Denny got out of prison, he did indeed claim invalidity payments for his back. Said he could not work but the social security people got suspicious and set out to watch him – and guess what?'

'He hasn't got a back injury,' said Romanes glumly.

'Spot on,' said the sergeant. 'They filmed him working in a supermarket warehouse. Lifting heavy boxes around. They were going to take him to court but settled for a warning and stopping his payments. That's why he bought his first shop. No one would employ a scammer like him after that. He was lucky that the supermarket took him with his record in the first place. It wasn't going to happen twice.'

'And now you think he's gone back to burgling?' said Romanes. He looked at Blizzard.

'Not for certain,' said Blizzard. 'But I think it's a possibility. From what we hear, his new shop is not doing very well and he may need the cash. And *if* he has gone back to burglary, and he *is* The Latch Man, he has no reason to suspect that we know about what happened with social security, does he? Like David keeps reminding me, it's all history.'

'Stupid, stupid,' said Romanes, slapping his forehead and looking at Allatt. 'We've been so stupid.'

'I wouldn't be too hard on yourselves,' said Blizzard. 'We did exactly what Denny meant us to do. We all took one look at him and wrote him off because of his back, didn't we? I certainly did – I know what it's like when my back flares up and I was prepared to believe him. Sympathise even.'

'But what made you think that Denny might be The Latch Man?' asked Allatt.

Blizzard thought back to Bill Gordon in his tidy little room at the home.

'Call it an old copper's instinct,' he said.

'So, what now?' asked Romanes.

'I want you and Sarah to find out as much as we can about him but keep it low key. He's a shrewd one, is Denny Buglass and I don't want him to get wind of what we're doing. And Sarah, contact the Met again, will you? I want De Montfort in custody before we lift Denny, if possible. He was Denny's fence back in the good old days and, if I'm right, they're back on the rob again.'

'Do you think that Denny committed the murder?' asked Romanes.

'*Murders*,' said Blizzard. 'Reynolds says that he thinks Doris Hornsby was murdered as well. But, no, I don't think that Denny killed either of them.'

'Then who–'

'I have one or two ideas. Nothing I'd like to put my name to yet, though.' Blizzard clapped his hands. 'Go on, let's get this cracked.'

Romanes and Allatt headed back to their desks. Chris Ramsey did not move.

'You wanted a word?' said Blizzard.

'Yeah, we've had another tip-off about the gunmen. An old dear reckons she saw a strange man in the back yard of the house next door. Haig Street this time. Back of the derelict carpet factory.'

'Yeah, I know it. What do you think? Another false alarm?'

'Wouldn't be the first, would it? We've had fifteen calls now. It's getting like Dodge City out there. Having said that, I don't really fancy going in without armed back-up just in case it is them. Trouble is, for some reason I can't get the heavy mob until tomorrow. No one will tell me why. Just something big in Broughton later today. Any idea what they're doing?'

'Keep it to yourself but they're going to lift a bunch of football hooligans.' Blizzard lowered his voice. 'Tommy Jacobs is running the op. He's been after them for months.'

'Why the cloak and dagger act?'

'One of the kids they're after is the son of a uniform superintendent at head office and he doesn't know anything about it. Tommy wants it to be a surprise in case he's tempted to tip his lad off. Blood and water and all that.'

'Makes sense,' said Ramsey. 'I'm happy to wait before we go in on Haig Street then. I can put it under surveillance in the meantime, if you're OK with that?'

'Fix it up and give me the details when you have them, will you? Anything else?'

'Sophie van Beek has been on from Rotterdam. The van involved in the firearms incident near their ferry port? Well, they've found some more CCTV. A couple of motorway cameras picked the vehicle up in Spain a day before it arrived at Rotterdam.'

'Spain? You sure?'

'Yeah, they tracked it back as far as the Costa del Sol and the cops there recognised the description as Geoff Hays.'

Blizzard looked pensive.

'What are you thinking?' asked Ramsey.

'That people will say I've gone mad.'

'Not sure anyone would dare say that. You've been right on everything else so far.'

'Yeah, I know. But this is different.' Blizzard gestured for the detective inspector to follow him out of the squad room. Once in the corridor, he looked round to make sure that they had not been followed. 'You see, I want you to check something out for me.'

Chapter twenty-five

'So, who are we going to see?' asked Blizzard. The inspector paused in the corridor as he and Colley approached his office.

'An old mate of mine. Jim Corbett. He's a detective sergeant with the Fraud Squad.'

'Not sure I've heard of him.'

'He transferred in from South Yorkshire a few weeks ago. He's spent most of his time with CID in Sheffield.'

'And how come you know him?'

'Been on a couple of courses with him but mainly from rugby. Played against him a few times. He's a fly half.'

'And that's supposed to mean something to me, is it?' They started walking again. 'He trustworthy?'

'Sound as a pound is Jim. Bit straight, like the DI, but I'd say that he's dependable. The fact that he's here suggests that he must have come up with something interesting. He sounded pretty excited on the phone. Well, as excited as he ever gets.'

They entered the office to find a smartly dressed officer sitting at the desk. He was wearing a beautifully pressed, expensive grey suit and a blue silk tie. Blizzard glanced at the equally immaculately attired Colley and raised an eyebrow.

'Jesus,' he muttered. He instinctively tightened the knot on his own half-mast tie. 'It's bad enough with Versace.'

Colley chuckled and Corbett looked at the chief inspector, unsure quite how to react.

'Don't worry,' said Colley. 'He's not always that welcoming.'

'Don't mind me,' said Blizzard. He extended a hand. 'Pleased to meet you, Jim.'

'I just hope I can help,' said Corbett. He was slightly awed by coming face-to-face with a detective whose fearsome reputation stretched right across the force. 'I think you'll find what I have interesting.'

'I'm sure we will,' said Blizzard. He sat down at his desk. 'Get us a tea will you, David?'

'Right-o. Do you want one, Jim?'

'Have you got camomile?' asked Corbett.

'Shouldn't think so,' said Colley.

'Raspberry?'

'Jesus Christ,' muttered Blizzard.

''fraid not,' said Colley.

'Then I'll just have hot water, thanks,' said Corbett.

Grinning at the chief inspector's unimpressed expression and Corbett's uncertainty, Colley scooped up the kettle and headed out into the corridor. Five minutes later, with the drinks made and mugs in hands, Blizzard nodded at the large pile of papers that Corbett had placed on his desk.

'And what are these?' asked the inspector.

'Records of financial transactions,' said Corbett. He took a sip of water. 'Dave suggested I check on Doris Hornsby and Edith Bradley – we're better than you when it comes to following the paper trail. I'm not surprised that Sarah struggled to find much. It's all very complex. Suffice to say that they were both extremely wealthy women.'

'Yeah, but we know that already,' said Blizzard.

'*Think* you know.'

'Hang on, we know that Doris Hornsby was worth seven or eight hundred thousand and that Edith left in the region of £350,000 when you count the cottage.'

'Chickenfeed,' said Corbett. 'Both of them had a damned sight more than that.'

'Really?'

'Doris and Edith's finances are divided into two. First, there's the transparent accounts, the ones you know about, the ones the Treasury and the taxman can see. The ones the solicitors can use for settling the wills. But that's only the half of it. Well, a third of it to be precise.'

Blizzard's eyes gleamed as he listened intently.

'See,' continued Corbett, 'there are other accounts offshore and Doris's had £2.5 million or so in them.'

'What!' exclaimed Blizzard. He looked at Colley in astonishment.

'It gets better,' said Corbett. He was enjoying the effect his words were having. 'Edith's hidden accounts had a couple of million in them as well.'

Blizzard said nothing for a few moments, shaking his head in disbelief. He took a sip of tea.

'Any idea where all this money was coming from?' he asked.

'It's a complicated set-up but both women seem to have received regular payments from Mexico. Mind you, from what I can see the accounts were originally set up in Spain and the money went walkabout after that.'

'Spain, eh? They weren't set up by Tony Bradley and Eric Leys, by any chance, were they?' asked Blizzard.

Colley looked at his boss in surprise.

'But they're dead,' said the sergeant.

'*Supposed* to be dead,' said Blizzard. 'What if they're not and they're our mysterious gunmen? I'd come back to Hafton for the thick end of five million.'

'But would you come back from the dead?' asked Colley.

'I've got Chris checking it with the cops in Spain.'

'Should have asked me. I can talk Spanish.' Colley pointed at an imaginary shop counter and said in a loud voice, 'Sandwicho, por favor!'

Blizzard raised his eyes to the ceiling.

'See what I have to work with, Jim?' he said.

'You have my sympathies,' said Corbett. 'However, neither of those names have cropped up in our enquiries. Having said that, if this is what we think it is, any name is bound to be false anyway. See, I'd say that your little old ladies were laundering drug money.'

'Agreed,' said Blizzard. He sat back and gave a shake of the head. 'A right couple of Ma Bakers!'

'And there's more,' said Corbett. 'A couple of weeks ago, Doris Hornsby's accounts were all closed down.'

'By whom?' asked Blizzard.

'Well, in theory, Doris did it.'

'In theory?'

'Yeah, but I don't believe that for one minute. Not least because the money was transferred to a number of accounts belonging to Martin Hornsby.'

Blizzard gave a look of intense satisfaction.

'Do you think that he set up the original accounts as well?' he asked. 'Is all this money really his?'

'Pretty sure it isn't, but I do think that he found out about it. Fairly recently, I'm guessing.'

'It's certainly a lot of motive to kill someone,' said Blizzard. He looked at Colley. 'Even your mother.'

'But is there not a danger that we are adding two and two and making five?' asked Colley. 'Maybe Doris told him about the cash and he worried that, because she was getting confused, he had to protect the money in case she did something daft – donated it all to the Battersea Dogs Home or something? After all, he's the one who famously turned his back on his family's involvement in crime. Maybe he's completely innocent.'

'Actually, I don't think he is that innocent,' said Corbett. 'See, I did a bit of digging into his business. He was known as a sharp operator was Martin Hornsby. Nothing illegal but he knew all the short-cuts. What *is* beyond doubt is that all Doris's money was transferred to him a couple of weeks ago.'

'Hang on,' said Blizzard, 'you said that Doris authorised the transfer. Martin may be a heel but nothing you have said proves anything illegal, surely? A smart lawyer would make mincemeat of us.'

'Except I reckon that Martin forged her signature on the transfer documents. I checked with the ones at her bank in Hafton. The signatures are very similar but I think that someone else did the ones on the transfer documents. I showed them to a handwriting expert and she agrees. Nope, what you have on your hands is a good old-fashioned fraud.'

'Excellent,' said Blizzard. He paused for a moment or two to digest what he had heard. 'Are you able to check if any attempts have been made to access Edith Bradley's accounts?'

'It's more complicated because she doesn't seem to have any close relatives but that is not to say that your man will not try something. Unless you nick him now…'

Chapter twenty-six

'We're close,' said Blizzard. 'I can feel it, Arthur. We are so bloody close.'

'Certainly a lot closer than we were,' said the superintendent cautiously. 'I'm just not quite sure what we are close to.'

They were sitting in Ronald's office, grabbing a late lunch of sandwiches and tea, during which the chief inspector had spent a quarter of an hour outlining his theories about the murders of Edith Bradley and Doris Hornsby.

'I grant you there is much we do not know,' said Blizzard. 'But, nevertheless, it is all beginning to come together. And I reckon we know enough to make our move. We have to start hauling people in.'

'You'll get no disagreement from me there,' said Ronald. He took a sip of tea and reached for his ham sandwich. 'The chief constable called again this morning, asking where we are with things.'

Chris Ramsey popped his head round the door.

'Sorry to disturb you,' he said. 'But the Spanish police have confirmed that Eric Leys and Tony Bradley *did* die in that car crash. They had ID on them and everything. There is no way they are still alive. Sorry.'

'It makes no difference,' said Blizzard. He jumped to his feet. 'Even if they *are* dead, it could be their associates who have come looking for the money. Anyway, for the moment, that is a secondary issue. OK, I'm off.'

'Let me know what happens,' said Ronald as Blizzard headed for the door.

The chief inspector, who had just rammed the last of his cheese sandwich into his mouth as he struggled into his suit jacket, nodded and disappeared into the corridor. He headed for the squad room where he picked up Colley. Before they left the police station, they looked in on Graham Ross's office door.

'Did you get the message?' said the inspector. 'I left a note on your desk.'

'Yes, I did,' said the forensics officer, looking at him unsurely. 'But we've done all that once.'

'Yeah, I know, now I want you to go back and do it again.'

'Yes, but–'

'But nothing, Graham. Go with me on this one.' Blizzard noted his expression. 'Look, I am not saying that forensics have slipped up, I am just saying that we might have been looking for the wrong thing.'

Ross shrugged.

'OK,' he said, 'but I think we will be wasting our time.'

'Then blame me,' said Blizzard and left the room.

* * *

Twenty-five minutes later, he and Colley were standing at the front door of a pleasant semi-detached house in western Hafton. It was another overcast and uncomfortably clammy afternoon and, while he waited for the door to open, Blizzard looked round at the neatly maintained garden with its immaculate borders and the flowers in neat lines. His mind turning gloomily to the bedraggled state of his own garden; he kept promising Fee that he'd get it sorted but somehow it never happened. Perhaps he'd take a few days off once this was all over. His thoughts were dragged back to more pressing matters when the door swung open and there stood Myra Hornsby. The detectives noted that her make-up was smudged with tears that glistened on her cheeks.

'Mrs Hornsby?' said Blizzard. He flashed his warrant card. 'Is your husband in?'

'No, he's not,' she said in a strained voice. She leaned heavily against the door frame. 'I don't know where he is.'

'May we come in?'

She hesitated for a moment then nodded weakly and stood aside. Martin Hornsby's house was as immaculate and precise as his garden, the hallway neat and uncluttered, the telephone directories lined up perfectly straight on the little occasional table and the dark-wood wall panels well polished. Myra gestured for the officers to go into the living room, which was as tidy as the hallway, the green three-piece suite beautifully maintained, the television dusted to within an inch of its life, the flowers in the vase on the gleaming sideboard carefully arranged. Myra sat down and took out a handkerchief which she used to dab at her eyes.

'Time for you to tell us what has been happening, I think,' said Blizzard.

'I don't know what you mean.'

'You can drop the act, Myra, we know that Doris was worth well more than three million.'

She looked at them in sheer amazement, her mouth gaping open.

'Three million?' she gasped. 'You must have made a mistake – she was worth much less than that.'

'Did Martin tell you that?' asked Colley.

'He said that we were going to have to sell the cottage at a much lower price than he had hoped. And he said that we'd lose a lot in inheritance tax as well. He said it would be enough to see us through our retirement as long as we weren't extravagant.' She gave a little smile. 'He said we might be able to buy a little cottage on the coast. It had always been our dream.'

'Well,' said Blizzard, 'I am afraid that he has been lying to you. Like I said, Doris was worth well over three million.'

'But how could she be?' she asked plaintively. 'Where did it all come from?'

'She had received a considerable amount of money from Spain over the years,' said Blizzard.

'Spain?' Myra looked bewildered.

'Yes, and it was the same for Edith Bradley. At first, we thought it was from their sons–'

'But the boys are dead,' blurted out Myra. 'They died in a car crash.'

'I know they did but someone was sending the money over and our inquiries have revealed that Martin has transferred it into his account. We think the someone has come looking for it.'

'No, this can't be true,' cried Myra. She slumped back in her chair. 'Martin would have told me. We always discussed everything. He would not do a thing like this!'

'I am afraid the evidence is conclusive,' said Blizzard. His voice softened as he watched her face crumple. 'And I am truly sorry that we had to be the ones to tell you.'

He meant it. It was the worst part of the job, exploding people's neat little lives by revealing the deceits of loved ones. Myra said nothing, sitting trying to digest the information then sobbing bitterly, realising that her neatly ordered life had been nothing but a cruel fantasy.

'Myra, I know this is hard for you,' said Colley, taking over from the chief inspector after she had regained some composure. 'However, we really do need to find your husband. He may be in danger. Do you have any idea where he might be?'

She shook her head.

'When did he go out?' asked the sergeant.

'This morning,' she said in a whisper.

'And how did he seem?' asked Blizzard.

'He'd not been the same since he heard that you had gone ahead with the exhumation. I have never seen him so upset. He said he was going out for a walk. When he did not come back for lunch, I knew that something was wrong – Martin was always in at 12.15 on the dot for his lunch. He likes to eat it with *Bargain Hunt*. He's always interested in what things cost.'

'So it would seem,' said Blizzard. 'And you have not heard from him since?'

'No.' She began to cry again. 'I am frightened that he might do something silly.'

'Silly?'

'Do away with himself. He seemed so very down. Nothing like his usual self.'

'Does he have anywhere he goes when he is worried?' asked Colley. 'A quiet place. A friend, perhaps?'

'No.' She shook her head. 'We always share everything. And he does not have any real friends. Just me.'

She looked at the detectives pathetically.

'Just me,' she repeated in a whisper. 'Just me…'

She lapsed into silence and they were acutely aware of the ticking of the clock on the mantlepiece. As Myra gazed blankly down at the carpet, the detectives left her to her thoughts and walked out into the front drive.

'Can you get someone over here?' said Blizzard. 'I think Myra needs watching.'

'Do you think she knows more than she is letting on?' asked the sergeant.

'It was a good act if she does.' Blizzard headed out on the pavement and turned towards his car. 'No, I think this was news to her. I wonder what else Martin did not tell her over the years. We need to get a major search organised for him.'

'Where do you think he is?'

'I reckon he's running as fast as he can,' said Blizzard. 'Because if we are right, some very nasty characters want their money back.'

As Blizzard got into the vehicle, the radio crackled.

'Control to Chief Inspector Blizzard,' said the disembodied voice. 'Please meet DC Allatt at Hayles Hotel, off Randall Street, where a body has been found.'

'But I have this awful feeling that we're too late,' said Blizzard quietly. He glanced back at the house, in the front window of which could be seen the silhouetted figure of a tearful Myra Hornsby. 'He should have stuck to the straight and narrow, after all.'

Chapter twenty-seven

The irony of the moment was not lost on John Blizzard and David Colley as they stood and surveyed the body in room eleven at the Hayles Hotel, the same room in which Bill Gordon had come so close to death when Gareth Robinson's gun jammed all those years before. It was a shabby place to die. The Hayles stood round the corner from the main railway station in the city centre but the word 'hotel' gave the establishment an allure that it hardly deserved. It was a dirty, grubby little guest house with grimy windows that looked like they had not been cleaned since Bill Gordon's day and tatty carpets that should have been replaced many years before.

The room was dark because the bright summer sunshine outside was partially blocked out by the body of a silhouetted man hanging in the window, his trouser belt twisted round his neck, his eyes lifeless in their sockets, the blue tongue lolling out of his mouth. A deep gash across his right cheek, from which oozed blood, suggested that he had fought his assailant before succumbing. The detectives stood and surveyed the man in silence for a moment. Sarah Allatt stood at the door, her face pale.

‘So,’ asked Blizzard at length. ‘What the hell is Denny Buglass doing here?’

‘Dunno,’ said Colley. He dragged his eyes away from the corpse and glanced round the room. ‘Do you know, I can’t think of a worse place to die.’

‘Have you ever thought of where you’ll meet your maker?’

The question surprised the sergeant and he looked at his boss in silence for a few moments.

‘What makes you ask that?’ he said eventually.

‘I’m not sure.’ Blizzard walked over to the window and peered closer at the belt. ‘I guess it’s becoming a dad and all that. Do you not feel the same thing from time to time?’

‘Every time I look at Laura, yes, but you can’t allow it to get in the way of you doing your job. If you did, you’d never turn up for work, would you?’

‘I guess not.’ Blizzard noted how the belt had been wrapped tightly round the window latch. ‘I don’t think that this is suicide, David. I reckon Denny was hanged from there deliberately as a message to us. It’s supposed to tell us that he was The Latch Man, just in case we hadn’t worked it out.’

‘I agree,’ said Colley. ‘But a message from whom?’

‘Presumably from whoever rented the room.’ The inspector turned to look at Allatt and noted her bloodless features. ‘You OK?’

‘It never gets any easier, does it?’

‘I am afraid not. Who found the body?’

‘A couple of the hotel girls,’ said Allatt. ‘They came round to clean the room and saw him hanging there. But take a look at the bed, guv. It’s not been slept in. I reckon that whoever did this rented the room specifically to lure Denny here.’

‘Sounds plausible,’ said Blizzard. ‘Do we know who *did* rent the room?’

There was a sound at the door and a timid-looking middle-aged man appeared, poorly shaven, wearing a shabby brown suit and desperately trying not to look at the body in the window. He waited at the door, rubbing his hands together nervously.

'The officer downstairs said you would want to talk to me,' he said.

'And you are?' asked Blizzard.

'Erroll Hayles. It's my hotel.'

'So, you can tell me who rented this room?' asked Blizzard.

'He called himself James Latch.'

The detectives exchanged significant glances.

'Latch?' asked Colley. 'Are you sure?'

'Yes, I thought it was a strange name but that is how he signed the register.' Hayles nodded to emphasise the point and a lock of lank black hair flopping across his eyes.

'Can you describe him?' asked the sergeant.

'Tall, slim, white hair, sixtyish. He looked very fit, like he looked after himself. And he was well dressed.'

'And the voice?'

'Southern, perhaps from London,' said the manager. 'Sounded well educated.'

'The man we saw in the railway station,' said Blizzard, looking at Colley. 'Did he say what he did for a living?'

'He said that he dealt in antiques.'

'A cut above your usual clientele, I would suggest, Mr Hayles.'

Hayles considered responding for a moment but thought better of it.

'And did he say why he was in Hafton?' asked Colley.

'For an antique jewellery fair at the Guildhall tomorrow. It's in the exhibition hall apparently.'

'Yes, well he lied to you,' said Blizzard. 'I just happen to know that there is no antiques fair at the Guildhall tomorrow because the room has been booked by the Hafton Model Railway Society for its annual exhibition. I was planning to take Mikey.'

* * *

The plainclothes officers sitting in the unmarked car in Haig Street were getting bored. They'd been there for several hours, watching a house in which nothing was happening.

'This is another false alarm,' said one of the officers. 'We're wasting our time here.'

'I suspect you're right,' said his colleague.

'You going to suggest we call it off?'

'Na, not yet. We'll give it another hour or so.'

* * *

Blizzard peered past Denny Buglass and out of the window, across the back yards of the terraced houses to the wasteland behind the railway station. If he looked hard enough, he could just make out the edge of the preservation society's shed. He sighed; what he wouldn't give for a couple of hours alone, working on the locomotive. Sensing that the others were expecting him to speak, he forced himself to focus on the job in hand and turned back into the room.

'And this man?' he asked. He gestured at Buglass. 'When did he arrive at the hotel?'

'The receptionist said he arrived this morning and came up here straight away.' Hayles clearly wanted to look anywhere but the window but found his eyes drawn to the dangling body.

'And was James Latch already there?'

'Yes.' Hayles shook his head vigorously, dislodging another lock of hair. 'He said he was expecting a visitor.'

'And no one heard anything?' asked Colley.

'There were a couple of bangs,' said Erroll.

'And you didn't try to find out what was happening?'

'You learn not to ask too many questions in this business.'

'What happened then?' asked Blizzard.

'Mr Latch left.'

'Alone?'

'Yes.'

'When?' asked Colley.

'About twenty minutes ago. He did not seem in a hurry or anything. He looked normal. I asked him if his friend was still in the room and he said he would be hanging around for the rest of the afternoon. I did not realise what he meant until…' Hayles' voice tailed off as he looked at the corpse.

'OK, thank you,' said Blizzard.

He watched the hotel owner scuttle gratefully out of the room. They could hear his feet clattering on the creaky stairs.

'This is unravelling,' said the inspector grimly. 'I want De Montfort and I want him now. He's clearly in Hafton.'

'Uniform are searching the streets for him,' said Allatt. 'And I've ordered roadblocks on all the main routes out of the city. I talked to the Transport Police at the railway station and Customs are keeping an eye on the airport for us.'

'Excellent work,' said Blizzard. 'We can't let him escape again.'

* * *

Back in Haig Street, one of the surveillance officers finished his crossword and threw the newspaper into the footwell.

'I'm going to have a closer look,' he said.

'The DI said to keep our distance.'

'Don't worry. I'll just stroll past the house. I won't stop or anything. No one will suspect a thing. Besides, there's no one in, is there?'

'I guess not. Be careful, though.'

'Will do.' The officer got out of the vehicle and strolled towards number twenty-five – which was when he glanced up and saw the handgun pointing out of the upstairs window.

Chapter twenty-eight

For a few moments after the gun was fired, time stood still in Haig Street. The surveillance officer cried out in alarm and threw himself to the ground as the bullet slammed into the window of the house opposite number twenty-five with a shattering of glass. He had not had enough time to gather his thoughts before the front door of number twenty-five itself was wrenched open and four men ran out into the street, one of them brandishing the handgun. Noticing the officer struggling to his feet, the gunman pointed the weapon at him.

'Stay back!' he snarled.

The officer hurled himself behind the nearest front wall and the men ran towards a red car parked nearby. One of them clambered into the driver's seat and turned the ignition key and the engine roared into life. With a squeal of tyres, the vehicle sped towards the end of the street just as a blue saloon careered round the corner. The vehicles collided with a renting of metal. For a few moments there was silence then the men spilled out of their vehicle. Two of them ran past the blue vehicle, which now had steam billowing from under the bonnet and whose front seat occupants were slumped forwards, and disappeared round the corner. The other two, including the gunman, made as if to follow but turned back when their way was blocked by a couple of patrol cars which slewed across the end of the street.

The men hesitated for a few moments then turned and ran back down Haig Street, towards number twenty-five. Another police vehicle turned into the street from the other end and the gunman loosed off another shot, which blew out one of the headlights. He aimed again but there was a click and, as two uniformed officers got out of the vehicle, the men dived back into number twenty-five and slammed the door behind them. Silence reigned for a few moments, then the air was filled with the wail of sirens.

Over at the Hayles Hotel, Blizzard and Colley had just got back into their vehicle when the radio coughed into life.

'Message for Chief Inspector Blizzard,' said a voice. 'DI Ramsey urgently requires you to attend Haig Street where shots have been fired at police.'

'It never rains,' said Blizzard with a sigh.

Within five minutes, he and Colley were on the scene of what had already turned into a siege. Uniformed officers were evacuating frightened residents from their homes and pushing people back behind a line at the end of the street, where a growing crowd watched in fascination, people craning their necks to catch a piece of the action. Beyond the line, several armed police officers were crouching behind parked cars, their guns trained on the house, from which no sound emanated. All its curtains were drawn.

Blizzard pushed his way through the crowd and walked to where Chris Ramsey was standing. He looked at the two wrecked cars, their front ends crumpled.

'What the hell happened, Chris?' demanded Blizzard. 'I thought the idea was to go in tomorrow.'

'Yeah, it was,' said the DI gloomily. 'But the people in the house spotted one of the surveillance officers and loosed off a shot from the upstairs window.'

'How come he let that happen?'

'Good question.'

'I take it they missed him?'

'Thank goodness.' Ramsey pointed to the shattered front window of the house opposite number twenty-five. 'A few minutes earlier and the old dear would have been on her way out to the shops.'

'How many of them were there?'

'Four. Came bowling out of the house and jumped into a car.' Ramsey pointed to the two wrecks. 'The red one.'

'Who was driving the blue one?' asked Blizzard. 'Is that one of ours?'

'It belongs to the other surveillance team.'

'Anyone injured?'

'Badly shaken up, that's all. Two of the crims ran into Elliston Street.' Ramsey gestured towards the road running across the top of Haig Street.

'And the other two are in the house?'

'Yeah. Their gun jammed. They've still got it.'

Blizzard surveyed the scene.

'So much for keeping it low-profile,' he said. He noticed a firearms officer walking up the street towards them, gun resting in the crook of his elbow. 'I see you got the cavalry, after all.'

'Yeah, but they're not happy.'

'*They're* not happy.'

The senior firearms officer walked up to them.

'What's the situation?' asked Blizzard.

'They're not moving. My advice would be to sit it out. Not that I want to do that because we have a big job on tonight but I don't think we have much in the way of options. From what I hear, this is a right royal fuck up.'

'Agreed,' said Blizzard. He turned back to the DI, who was looking ever more miserable. 'What do we know about them, Chris?'

'The two that ran into Elliston Road were in their thirties but the two in the house are much older. They had grey hair, apparently.'

Blizzard gave a thin smile – his instincts were talking to him again. Ramsey noticed the gesture.

'You're still not thinking–?' he began.

'That's exactly what I'm thinking, Chris.'

'But they're dead!'

Blizzard looked towards number twenty-five.

'Are they?' he said.

Leaving a bemused Ramsey to ponder the comment, Blizzard walked to where Colley was standing, talking to some of the neighbours behind the police cordon.

'Anything new?' asked the inspector.

'Control have just been on. Marion Rowbotham has been making a pest of herself. Wondering if it's true that you told Janice and Robert that Doris was murdered? And she was asking how we're doing with our investigation. What do you want me to do?'

'Can you get Sarah to pick her up?' *Marion knows everything.* 'If we're right, her criminal history is not as far behind her as we might have thought. And tell Sarah to take back-up, will you? These people are dangerous.'

'These people? She's a pensioner!'

'Don't talk to me about sodding pensioners,' said Blizzard.

* * *

An hour later, Blizzard and Ramsey were still standing in Haig Street, surveying the house. A little further down the street, deep in conversation, stood Arthur Ronald and the deputy chief constable, who had abandoned a meeting at headquarters and driven down to the city with a blue-light escort to oversee the operation. Another car arrived with flashing blue lights and the assistant chief constable got out.

'Bloody hell,' said Blizzard. 'Any more brass and we'll have to start a band.'

Colley heard the comment and gave a low laugh. Ramsey smiled for the first time since he had arrived on the scene.

'Any word from Sarah?' asked Blizzard.

'No sign of Marion Rowbotham at home,' said Colley. He chuckled as he watched Ronald intercept the assistant chief constable and guide him over to where the deputy was standing, rather in the way he would small children. 'Boy, he's good, is Arthur. Re Marion, they're doing house-to-house in the village now.'

'I'm not sure they'll find her,' said Blizzard. 'She's had it away on her toes. No wonder she kept cropping up in our inquiries.'

The detectives stood and watched Ronald and the top brass engage in animated conversation for several minutes. Both the deputy and the chief looked unhappy at what they were hearing.

'Too many cooks,' said Ramsey.

'Hopefully not,' said Blizzard.

Discussion over, Ronald walked across to them.

'OK, John,' he said. 'They're not happy about you trying to talk them out, but they've agreed that it's your show. Just make sure that you're right. We could end up looking pretty stupid if you're not.'

'Talk them out?' exclaimed Ramsey. 'We should let firearms handle it. What if they've got the gun working again? Can't you talk some sense into him, sir?'

'When did that ever happen?' said Ronald.

'Your concern is touching,' said Blizzard. He started walking towards the police tape. 'But I'll be fine. See you in a few minutes.'

'Be careful, John,' said Colley. 'Think of Fee and the little 'un.'

Blizzard looked back at him – it was very rare that the sergeant used his first name while they were working.

'I will,' he said. 'Promise.'

He walked down the street and nodded at the firearms inspector who handed him a megaphone.

'Now listen,' said the firearms inspector. 'This is against my advice but I have been outranked. Just remember that this isn't the Wild West and you're not John Wayne so no heroics – and don't get too close. No further than number thirty-two, the one on the other side with the green door. You may be wearing Kevlar but you can still get shot. Understand?'

'Yeah.'

'And I'll be right behind you.'

'I don't want anyone else put at ri–'

'My gun's bigger than yours,' said the firearms inspector. 'Don't argue.'

Blizzard gave him a grateful look.

'Thank you,' he said.

The gathering watched Blizzard stroll nonchalantly down the street, trying to look as calm as he could and pausing outside the green door as instructed. The firearms inspector followed a few paces behind. For a moment, it looked as if Blizzard was about to take a further step but a sharp look from the inspector cautioned him against it. It was funny, thought Blizzard as he stood and surveyed the siege house, something had changed within him over the couple of years since he had taken up with Fee. He had been in plenty of tight spots over the years but, through it all, he had experienced a strange fatalism, a feeling that were this to be his day to die then he would accept it without demur. He did not feel like that now; as Colley had reminded him, now there was something new and exciting to live for: Fee, the baby. Now, there was an awful lot to lose. And now, whereas previously a deep calm had descended upon him in such situations, he could feel the blood pounding in his head and his hands were shaking and sweating.

'Becoming almost human,' he muttered.

'John Blizzard human?' said the firearms inspector. 'Who'd have thought it? Hey, not too close. We don't want Butch Cassidy and the Sundance Kid to have a pop at you, do we now?'

'Don't you watch anything else but old Westerns?'

'Just be careful,' said the inspector with a smile.

'I'll bear it in mind,' said Blizzard. He liked this man. It was as if, despite the watching crowds, no one else existed in the world at that moment but the two of them. It was then that Blizzard realised that he did not even know who he was. 'What's your name?'

'Matt. Matt Sparkbrook.'

'Well, Matt Sparkbrook,' said Blizzard. He glanced at the house nervously. 'Thanks for being here.'

He glanced down and clicked on the megaphone.

'Tony!' he shouted. 'Tony Bradley! Eric Leys! This is Detective Chief Inspector John Blizzard. Throw your weapon out of the window and come out with your hands where we can see them. If you co-operate, you will not be hurt.'

There was no reaction.

'It's got to end here,' shouted Blizzard. 'Too many people have lost their lives already!'

There was silence for a minute then an upstairs curtain twitched and a face appeared at the sash window and furtively looked up and down the street. Within a second, it had ducked back out of sight but it was enough for John Blizzard. Despite the greying hair, the wrinkles of the passing decades and the tanned skin after years in the Spanish sun, there was no mistaking the strong cheekbones and prominent nose of the Leys family. Blizzard had seen them in Martin, had seen them in Robert and he had seen them in old photographs of George. Before, it had been a hunch, now Blizzard knew that he was right. Eric Leys had come home – and that meant Tony Bradley was with him.

A few moments later, the front door to the house swung open and, if the inspector craned his neck, he could just make out two figures in the shadows of the hallway. He took a few steps further and saw Matt Sparkbrook tense. The same was true of the other firearms officers ranged along the street, their grips tightening just a fraction on the triggers. This was a dangerous time, the chief inspector knew, that moment during which all the training for these officers came into its own, when theory became reality, when it was all down to human nature – when the cut-out figures popping up on the firing range became flesh and blood and armed and dangerous at that. The moment when armed officers had to make the instant decision that was the difference between life and death. And that life and death, realised Blizzard, could be his own if this went down wrong. One mistake, one fraction's panic…

Nevertheless, in that split second, he had time to examine the man who now emerged from the front door. The years had been kind to Eric Leys. Dressed in an expensive grey designer suit with white shirt but no tie and shiny black shoes, he was lithe and looked fit and strong; the overall impression was of a man much younger than his years. He surveyed the street calmly, taking in the armed officers then looking over to the excited crowds being ushered further back by uniformed officers.

Seconds later, Tony Bradley emerged, carrying a handgun down by his side. The years had not been as kind to the former enforcer. The face, beneath wispy greying hair, was chubby and he was sweating profusely as he surveyed the scene with his piggy eyes. To Blizzard's alarm, there was none of the coolness that Eric was displaying; instead he could be seen for what he was, an instinctive thug whose life had been one of violence, a life which, if he was not careful, would end in the same way. Dressed in a black T-shirt straining to contain his stomach and ragged jeans, his portly frame confirmed a man for whom the muscle of those halcyon days as George Leys' enforcer was long gone to be replaced by the flab of too many years of high living. Bradley's fingers wrapped round the handgun just that little bit tighter. Blizzard glanced to his right and saw that the movement had not been lost on Matt Sparkbrook, whose eyes narrowed as he levelled his gun at the two men.

'Be careful,' he murmured.

Blizzard nodded, took a step forward and lifted the megaphone to his mouth again.

'It's over, boys,' he said. 'No more summer holiday.'

Bradley's arm twitched and he raised the handgun, loosing off a single shot before a crash reverberated round the street and six bullets cut him down, each one slamming into his body and sending him tumbling to the floor, blood spurting from gaping wounds. Blizzard had hurled himself to one side when the bullet was fired from the handgun and heard it fizz above his head and smash into the wall of the house behind him, showering him with fragments of brickwork. As the chief inspector hit the ground, he was vaguely aware of terrified screams from the crowds at both ends of the street and the pounding of boots as officers ran towards him.

Eric Leys stood as if transfixed, gazing down open-mouthed at his friend as he writhed on the ground for a few moments then, with a feeble gurgle and a final twitch, was still. For a moment, it looked as if Eric would make a grab for the gun now lying at his friend's side but a barked command from Matt Sparkbrook halted his almost imperceptible movement and, moments later, he was being roughly handcuffed by firearms officers.

Colley, meanwhile, had rushed over to where the chief inspector sprawled on the pavement.

'Are you alright, guv?' he exclaimed.

An ashen-faced Blizzard struggled to his feet, readily taking the sergeant's arm for support, and nodded weakly.

'Yeah, I think so,' he said. He glanced behind him at the shattered brickwork and a thought struck him. 'I don't suppose there's any way we can keep this from Fee, is there? She'll never come back to work at this rate.'

Colley looked over at the crowds of onlookers, at the television crews and the news photographers.

'Do you know,' he said. 'I don't think there is.'

Chapter twenty-nine

'You look pretty fit for a man who died many years ago,' said Blizzard. 'Death obviously suits you, Eric.'

'I try to look after myself.'

It was late afternoon and the inspector and Colley were sitting in the cramped interview room at Abbey Road Police Station, opposite their prisoner. Eric Leys had said nothing on his arrival, clearly deeply shocked by the death of his friend and glowering at any officer who spoke to him. But now, sitting at the table, he was much more composed and having declined the presence of a solicitor, he finally looked in the mood to talk.

His face clouded over.

'Before I talk to you, I need to know something,' he said. 'I know that you exhumed my mother. Was she murdered?'

'How do you know that she was exhumed?' asked Blizzard.

'I hear things. *Was* she murdered?'

'Doris was murdered, yes,' said Blizzard. 'I am sorry to be the one to tell you that.'

Eric digested the information for a moment; tears glistened in his eyes. He wiped them away with the back of his hand.

'She did not deserve that,' he said. 'Any idea who did it?'

'I was rather hoping that you could help us with that.'

'I hope you are not insinuating that I killed my mother.'

'Well, did you?'

'Oh, come on!' exclaimed Eric. His anger seemed genuine. 'Why would I do that? Besides, I was not even in the UK when she died.'

'You could have had someone do it for you. Look at it from our point of view. You turn up alive and well just as your mother dies and just as, presumably, you discover that she has transferred the money to Martin. How were you to know he had forged her signature? Maybe you thought that she had betrayed you? Maybe you took your revenge on her?'

'A nice little theory,' said Eric. He was calm again.

'Is it just a theory, though? Maybe Tony assumed his mother was in on it as well. Maybe you killed them both.'

'We may be villains, but we'd never do anything like that.' Leys gave a slight smile. 'Why, even the Krays were kind to their mother.'

'You can quit the loving son routine, Eric. I know exactly what the two of you are like and you're no Kray Twins. However, when it comes to the money that was stolen–'

'Our money, Chief Inspector. Not the money, *our* money. Our mothers were just looking after it for us. Respectable little old widows excite less interest than a couple of likely lads from Spain.'

'But I think you'd do anything to protect it. It all fits, Eric.'

'You sound like Bill Gordon.' Eric sat back in his chair and allowed a smile to creep across his face. 'He made a lot of things fit, did Bill, but somehow I can't see you doing that, Chief Inspector. You're better than that. And for the record, we realised that Martin had faked my mother's signature and that she had no idea what he was up to.'

'But you can see why we think like this, can't you?' said Blizzard. 'You don't see your mothers for years then suddenly you turn up when the murdering begins. It's a remarkable coincidence.'

'It would be were it not for the fact that we saw our mothers regularly over the years.'

'In Spain?'

'Sometimes, yes. They enjoyed nice holidays there, Mum was partial to a couple of glasses of red – but we also met over here.'

Blizzard looked surprised.

'Here?' he said.

'Doubtless you know that my mother and Edith used to meet up for tea every so often? Well, sometimes they had friends round as well. A couple of old dears.'

'So?'

'It's amazing what you can do with a wig and a headscarf,' said Eric with a knowing smile. 'So, you see, Chief Inspector, you might have assumed that we have been bad sons, but the truth is we never lost contact – and we saw them alright for money as well. Ever wondered how Edith could afford to live in a nice village like that when her husband worked for the council?'

'Did Martin know that you were still alive?' asked Colley.

'That straight-laced bastard?' exclaimed Eric. 'If he'd known that, he'd have called you lot that fast.'

'Perhaps he did find out, though,' said Blizzard. 'Perhaps you killed *him*. He's gone missing.'

'He's missing with our money then. And no, we didn't kill him. That's not to say we would not have been tempted if we had caught up with him.'

'OK, Eric, better tell us the story from the beginning,' said Blizzard. He settled back in his seat. 'From when your dad was shot and you and Tony legged it.'

Leys paused for a moment, his mind transported back to a wicked night in Hafton, to a rainswept street and three men emerging from the pub after a heavy night drinking. Three men who wielded immense power, who had made fortunes from their illegal activities, who struck fear into the hearts of those with whom they dealt, men who commanded immense loyalty from their acolytes. Three men laughing and joking drunkenly but moments away from an incident that would alter the face of crime in Hafton in ways still being felt years later. A brutal incident that blew apart the most successful crime family the city had known.

'We had been drinking at The Elephant.' Eric's suave veneer had crumbled, his voice quiet and displaying strain for the first time. 'It was *our* boozer. Everyone knew it. There was no reason to hide it; we never dreamt that anyone would dare take us on. No one messed with George Leys and the boys. It was not difficult for them to find us.'

'And who were *they*?' asked Blizzard.

'A London gang run by a scumbag called Tommy Fearnley. We'd done some business together – we sold them some guns for a couple of bank jobs – and they got it into their heads that we could be partners. When we refused, Fearnley decided to muscle in on our patch. Finding us was easy enough.'

'Then what happened?'

'We came out about midnight,' recalled Eric, his voice soft. 'There was me, Dad and Tony. We didn't see the car until it was too late. Big black thing it was, that's all I remember of it. Driven by a bloke called Robinson. Fearnley's hitman.'

He shook his head in disbelief.

'We never thought they'd do it,' he said. 'We really didn't. Dad was dead by the time he hit the ground. It was too dangerous for me and Tony to stay in Hafton after that. Dad was a warning. If we had refused to play ball – and we would have – they would have come back for us. We panicked. Got out of the city that night.' He smiled sadly. 'Just left Dad lying there, Chief Inspector. Can you believe that? Just left him in the gutter.'

'And you fled to Spain?'

'Yeah, we had some contacts out there. We changed our names, hooked up with some of the expats, started dealing drugs, got rich.' Leys held out the lapels of his jacket. 'This kind of gear doesn't come cheap, you know.'

He looked at Blizzard's dishevelled suit.

'I can give you the number of my tailor, if you want,' he said impishly.

Blizzard said nothing. He thought of Jim Corbett's expensive suit, thought of Versace's silk ties, and glanced across at the immaculately attired Colley. The sergeant knew what his boss was thinking and gave the slightest of winks. Blizzard gave him a rueful look and returned his attention to the prisoner.

'No, thanks,' he said. 'Why stay out there? As I understand it, the London gang was running scared after killing your father. And the police got the shooter anyway. Surely, you would have been safe in Hafton?'

'From Fearnley, maybe, but not from your lot. He was a crafty old beggar was Bill Gordon. He'd have found something to pin on us. He knew all the short-cuts. It would not have been too difficult. When folks knew that we had left Hafton, they were lining up to talk to the police. We decided it was safer to do a Ronnie Biggs and stay away.'

'But you did see your mothers, though,' said Colley.

'Course we did. All those holidays Mum and Edith used to take on the South Coast? They used to book a guest house in Eastbourne and stay there for a couple of nights just in case Bill Gordon's boys were following them and go and play bingo or whatever until the surveillance officers got bored. Then off they'd go.' He chuckled. 'Off to Sunny Spain, tra la la la la la.'

Colley allowed himself a smile.

'But why risk the visits home?' asked Blizzard.

'We wanted to see our dear old mums. Wear a bit of slap and talk a bit of business over fruit scones and a pot of tea. We could pass ourselves off at a distance. Mind, can't say I look my best in a headscarf. And as for Tony in a wig…'

Colley smiled again. Whatever his criminal history, it was difficult not to like Eric Leys. His easy-going manner contrasted sharply with his brother's uptight approach to life. The sergeant rebuked himself inwardly, thinking of the man's many victims over the years.

'As far as we know, no one ever cottoned on,' continued Leys. 'We got the odd strange look from the neighbours but I don't think they ever worked it out. If they did, they thought it better to keep their mouths shut. Marion Rowbotham might have known. She saw me in the road outside mother's one time and gave me an odd look.'

'You knew each other, I think?'

'From the old days. Her dad was one of our drivers. Marion used to knock about with Denny Buglass and some of the other boys. He had a bit of a thing about her. Not that it ever came to much. She had more class than Denny.'

'He worked for you as well, I think?' asked Blizzard.

'Yeah, if we needed a break-in doing, he was the man. They didn't come any better than Denny Buglass.'

'Anyone else know you were alive?' asked Blizzard. 'Your kids, for instance?'

'No comment. And don't press me on it. You keep them out of this.'

Silence settled on the room for a few moments.

'So, when did you last see your mothers?' asked the inspector eventually.

'About three or four years ago when they announced that they were too old for travelling. We knew that if we wanted to keep seeing them, we would have to come over here. We decided against it. Everyone's luck runs out some time.' Eric paused. 'Like Tony's did today.'

There was silence for a moment as he stared at the table without speaking. The officers let him compose his thoughts.

'And you haven't come over since?' asked Blizzard.

'I was thinking about it then Mum said she could not see me anymore. I got the impression that it was something to do with Martin.' His face assumed a fierce expression. 'He may do the holier than thou act but he's a nasty piece of work, is my brother. Mum said he was round the house all the time. He'd have been bound to find out that we were alive if we tried to see her. We couldn't risk that.'

'So how come you are here now?' said Blizzard.

'We needed to find out what had happened to the money.'

'Our financial guys have tracked it through Mexico. Why Mexico?'

'We moved there a few years ago. Our wives are there and Tony's got a couple of kids.' He shook his head. 'Someone will have to tell them what has happened.'

'We'll sort that,' said Blizzard.

Leys nodded his thanks.

'Why leave Spain?' asked Colley.

'The Spanish police were getting heavy with expats and the last thing we wanted was for our money to go into the benevolent fund… if you get my drift.' Leys patted his back pocket. 'Spain's no different from here…'

'I hope you are not suggesting there are bent cops in Hafton?' said Blizzard sharply.

'Ask yourself why Bill Gordon and his sergeant always drove nice big motors.'

Blizzard did not reply.

'So, who died in the car crash?' asked Colley.

'Couple of winos. Don't know their names. We got them pissed, Tony jammed the accelerator and they smashed into the tree. He had primed the car so it would explode. It was in his name, we left my driving licence lying on the road like it had been thrown clear and the bodies were so badly burned that everyone assumed it was us.'

'But didn't the Spanish police suspect anything?' asked Colley.

'We were off their hands and that was all that bothered them. We've been lifted a couple of times over the years but no one has ever made the connection.' Leys looked at Blizzard. 'It was a real shock when we heard you shouting our names earlier.'

'And the other two men with you, who are they?' asked the inspector. 'We know one of them is Lawson.'

'Yeah, he handled things for us in Spain. Came over to help us out if things got heavy. The other guy owns a few houses in Hafton so we used some of them to hide out.'

'And what was the plan?' asked Blizzard. 'Kill Martin?'

'If he's dead, we didn't do him.'

'No, I don't think you did.'

Chapter thirty

'Did you know that your father and Tony Bradley were still alive?' asked Blizzard.

'What did Dad say?' asked Janice.

'Nothing.'

Blizzard and Colley were sitting in Janice's living room. It was still light, the evening was warm and the children were playing in the garden, squealing with delight in the lengthening summer shadows as they splashed each other with water in the paddling pool. Their mother was sitting on the sofa, fighting back tears, and Robert was staring out of the window without speaking as usual. Janice followed his gaze, checking that the children were alright. However, Robert appeared to be staring past his niece and nephew into the middle-distance, focused on nothing in particular.

'So, *did* you know?' asked Blizzard.

'Yes,' said Janice at length. 'Yes, we did. Dad probably said nothing in order to protect us. He said we could be committing a criminal offence. He did not want us to go to prison.'

'And I take it you've seen him?'

'A few times down the years. We had some nice holidays. Even went out to Mexico, didn't we, Rob?'

Rob nodded. Janice looked out of the back window to the children, who were still splashing each other with water.

'Dad got to meet his grandchildren,' she said with a gentle smile. 'He was thrilled to bits. He loves playing with them.'

Blizzard sat and surveyed her for a moment. The stark contrast in the lives of villains had always fascinated him, how men capable of acts of cruelty and violence could also lavish such tender care and affection on their loved ones. Some would say it was the only redeeming feature in people like Eric Leys and Tony Bradley. Blizzard would probably have resisted the temptation to agree, on principle. Colley, had he been asked, would have taken a softer line, his enduring faith in human nature usually allowing him to find some positives in most people, however small.

'Dad is very important to the kids,' continued Janice. 'It was like something was missing in their lives until they met him. His new wife is very kind. Mum died before the kids were born and my ex-husband's parents don't really bother. I never got on with them. They don't even send anything for the kids at Christmas.'

Blizzard raised an eyebrow.

'The divorce was very acrimonious,' explained Janice. 'They blamed me. So, finding out they had a grandad was amazing for the kids. At first, we were worried that they would tell someone and give the game away but they kept the secret.'

She glanced out of the window.

'Bless them,' she said. 'You see, apart from Granny and their Uncle Robbie, there really has been no one else in the family over here. They love their Uncle Robbie, he's such a softie with them…'

Robert looked suitably embarrassed.

'…but meeting their grandad, that was something special,' Janice concluded wistfully. 'So very special.'

'Didn't you think to tell us all of this?' asked Blizzard. 'It would have put things in a different light.'

'You would only have arrested Dad. Martin would have loved that.'

'I am sure he would,' said Blizzard. 'We need to find him. He's gone missing and Myra does not know where he might be. Have you any ideas?'

'Why ask us?' said Janice. 'We'd be the last people to know.'

'Why do you want him anyway?' asked Robert. 'Do you think he was the one who killed Granny?'

'It's more complicated than that,' said Blizzard.

* * *

Graham Ross and the forensics team had spent several frustrating hours searching Doris Hornsby's cottage again. Eventually, a couple of the team walked up to Ross, who was staring moodily out of the living room window into the back garden as the evening shadows lengthened.

'We're wasting our time here,' said John Ferris. 'I don't understand why Blizzard asked us to do this.'

'Because he wants to make sure that we did not miss anything.' Ross gestured to the sofa. 'Let's review what we've got, then call it a day.'

They sat down.

'Let's start with fingerprints,' said Ross.

'Well, we found plenty of them,' said Ferris. 'But we checked them all out after we'd done the initial search. Most of them belonged to Martin, the nurse and Doris herself.'

He looked at his colleague.

'There were some more, weren't they?' he said. 'But they all checked out as well, didn't they?'

'They did,' she said. 'Some were from Janice and Robert and some were those of children, which we presume to be Janice's kids. Oh, and there were also some belonging to the neighbours who used to help Doris. They were all older prints, dating from the time before Martin banned visitors. We found them in places which had escaped the duster.'

'Yeah,' said Ferris. 'But we eliminated every one of them. Everyone had legitimate reasons to be there.'

'As far as I can see,' said Ross, 'we did everything right here.'

'Not quite,' said a voice.

They turned to see team member Andy Green standing at the door from the kitchen, a grim expression on his face.

'What do you mean?' asked Ross.

'Blizzard was right. We did miss something. *I* missed something. There's something you need to see.'

Green led them out of the back door and towards a ramshackle shed at the bottom of the garden.

'We searched this, surely?' said Ross.

'Yeah, I did it.' Green led the way into the shed and pointed to an old oak sideboard against which leaned a yard brush, dusty and caked in grime.

'I've not seen that before,' said Ross.

'I have. I found it at the time. It was lying under some old carpet with a load of other tools.'

'So?'

'There's a print on it.'

'Surely, you picked it up at the time, though?'

'I checked it, yes, but did not realise the significance.'

'And what *is* the significance?' asked Ross.

'Well, I assumed it was quite old because of the muck but I have just checked with one of the neighbours. They remembered seeing Martin arriving with it the day he bought it. Three months ago.'

'So?'

'Well, that means that whoever's print it was, was in the house recently, doesn't it?'

'It does, yes.' Ross was starting to experience a sickly sensation in the pit of his stomach.

'What's more, when I looked closer, I found a couple of shards of glass in the bristles,' said Green. 'Easy to miss but they're the same as the glasses in the kitchen cupboard. That means that the brush was used to clean up a smashed glass – and they were the kind of glasses in which Doris had her water when she took her sleeping pills. I think there's a good chance that the print belongs to whoever killed her.'

'Don't tell me.' Ross closed his eyes. 'Martin Hornsby?'

'It's more complicated than that,' said Green.

* * *

'Complicated?' asked Janice. Tears started in her eyes. 'How complicated?'

'It's just complicated,' said Blizzard. 'There still remain questions to be answered about your grandmother's death.'

His mobile phone rang and he fished it out of his jacket pocket.

'I'm sorry about this,' he said.

Blizzard walked out into the hallway, shutting the door behind him, leaving the three of them sitting in uncomfortable silence, Janice fighting back the tears, Robert staring out of the window to where the children were still playing happily, impervious to the drama unfolding.

Colley followed his gaze. Damn, thought the sergeant as he watched the children, why couldn't they stay that age for ever and avoid all the nastiness of the world? If he was honest, that was one of the reasons why he had not been keen that he and Jay start a family – the realisation that his child would grow up in such a vicious world. But, every time he thought that way, and that included now, the sergeant reminded himself that coppers had warped views of the world and that most people never met a murderer, never saw a gun and would have no idea what a wrap of heroin looked like. However, as he sat in Janice's sun-dappled living room, it was difficult to banish the gloomy thoughts. The sergeant knew what was about to happen.

He had plenty of time to ruminate because the chief inspector was out of the room for the best part of five minutes. They could see him through the glass in the door as he paced round the hallway, deep in conversation. When the call finished, he slipped his phone back into his pocket, paused for a moment to compose his thoughts, gave a heavy sigh, closed his eyes for a moment then re-entered the room. Three faces turned to him. Janice looked increasingly anxious, Robert's eyes were hooded and dark and Colley raised an enquiring eyebrow. Blizzard nodded then looked at Janice.

'I am sorry about this, I truly am,' he said.

Colley stood up.

'Robert Leys,' he said, 'I am arresting you on suspicion of the murder of Doris Hornsby.'

Robert's mouth fell open in shock and Janice stared at the sergeant in disbelief then burst into tears. Colley noticed, out of the corner of his eye as he put the handcuffs on Robert's wrists, that the children were still playing happily in the garden.

Chapter thirty-one

'So,' said Blizzard. He looked at Robert Leys, who was eying him balefully across the table. 'It seems that we were looking at the wrong uncle all the time. We were looking at nasty Uncle Martin when we should have been looking at nice Uncle Robbie.'

'I ain't saying nothing,' said Leys.

It was shortly after eight that evening and the detectives were sitting in the interview room at Abbey Road. On the opposite side of the table sat Robert Leys and his lawyer Edgar Cole, a plump man with a shiny head and fleshy cheeks, who would rather have been at home with a glass of wine and was keen to get proceedings over with. As far as he was concerned, either his client admitted the lot quickly or refused to speak at all and the detectives adjourned proceedings until the morning. Whichever way, he did not really mind, a feeling strengthened by the brusque way Robert Leys had treated him in their brief chat before the interview began.

'My client has made it clear that he will not be making any statement,' said Cole. 'So, you had better charge him or let him go so we can all go home.'

'He does not need to say anything,' said Blizzard. He eyed the lawyer with his customary distaste for members of the legal profession. 'We know everything anyway.'

'Then perhaps you would like to charge him,' said the lawyer. He glanced at his watch. 'Because he is not going to co-operate with this interview. Indeed, from the little that he *has* communicated to me, he will strenuously deny the murder of his grandmother, whom he loved deeply.'

'Yeah, you're bluffing,' said Robert. 'I ain't saying nothing.'

'Then let me say it for you,' said Blizzard. 'We found your fingerprint on the brush.'

Leys went pale and Blizzard smiled slightly as he detected the first signs of a crack in his carefully constructed façade. One hard shove and it would come crashing down.

'Let me explain,' said the inspector, 'I had begun to wonder if we might not be focusing too much on Martin. Somehow, murder didn't quite seem his style, so we searched your grandmother's house again. That's how we found the fingerprint, which means that we can place you in the house and prove that there was some kind of struggle in which a glass was smashed, which you cleared up. I think you went there to rob her, Robert. You tried to give her an overdose of her sleeping pills, she disturbed you and you smothered her.'

'That's ridiculous!' exclaimed Robert. However, this time the voice wavered slightly and the look of defiance had gone. 'Bloody fairy stories. Why on earth would I do that?'

'Enlighten him, will you, Sergeant?'

'We have been talking to someone that I think you know. Raymond Buglass.'

Robert looked sick.

'And, pray, who is he?' asked the lawyer.

'We arrested him for burglary. Turns out that he and your client know each other because they drink at The Red Lion.'

'That proves nothing,' said the lawyer. 'I imagine a lot of people drink there.'

'You are right,' said Colley. 'They do. Except that the more we looked into the pub, the more we found. It turns out that The Red Lion has started a network for villains. It works like this: some of them bring in information about vulnerable victims, some of them do the burglaries and some fence the gear. It's a one-stop shop. All very enterprising. Raymond Buglass is one of those who does the burgling.'

'That does not mean that my client was involved,' said the lawyer. However, he was acutely conscious that he was losing all influence over the situation and his hopes of an early finish were fading rapidly.

'No, it does not,' said Colley. 'Except that we also discovered that, rather like Raymond Buglass, our Mr Leys has a problem with a moneylender called Jackie Rowlands. It seems that Jackie lent Robert money for drugs just as he did Raymond – all at extortionate interest rates, of course. You can probably guess how Jackie Rowlands likes to get his money back, Mr Cole. I'll give you a clue, it isn't a letter from head office on headed notepaper.'

Robert closed his eyes and the lawyer looked gloomy.

'Our investigation,' continued Colley, 'has revealed that Robert mentioned to the boys in The Red Lion that his grandmother had some expensive antique jewellery. We think he decided to steal it and the boys would fence it. We think he killed her because she could identify him.'

There was silence in the heavy atmosphere of the interview room.

'Once a Leys always a Leys, eh, Robert?' said Blizzard.

Robert eyed him for a moment then, to their astonishment, started to sob.

'I take it we are right?' said Blizzard softly.

Robert nodded dumbly, tears wracking his body.

'But I did not mean to kill her,' he said, voice cracked. 'I loved her. She was one of the few people who was ever decent to me.'

'Might I suggest–' began the lawyer.

'Might I suggest you let your client speak,' said Blizzard sharply.

The lawyer sat back in his chair, shrugged and said no more.

'So, Robert,' said Blizzard. 'Was it like Sergeant Colley described?'

'I was desperate.' Tears now rivered Robert's cheeks. 'Jackie threatened to cut up Janice's kids.'

He buried his head in his hands.

'I couldn't allow that to happen,' he said in a voice that was hardly audible. 'I'd do anything for them. Believe me, if I hadn't got the money, Jackie *would* have gone for the kids. I was already on borrowed time.'

'Is that why you went there twice?'

Robert nodded again.

'The first time I broke in, she woke up,' he said. 'I lost my bottle, gave a little bow and left. It was all I could think of to do. I reckoned it was such a ludicrous thing to do, everyone would think she was making it up. Dreaming.'

'It damn near worked,' said Blizzard. 'Did your grandmother recognise you?'

'If she did, she said nowt. I waited for you to arrest me, but nothing happened.'

'So, you went back?'

'Yeah. Things were getting really heavy with Rowlands. I needed that jewellery and I thought you'd blame it on The Latch Man anyway. I was looking through the drawers and she woke up…'

His voice tailed off, the horror of the moment stark in his mind.

'She stared straight at me,' he said, his voice a croak. 'Then she said my name. Said we were all against her.'

'And you did what?'

'Said I was here to give her a sleeping pill. She was so confused she seemed to believe me. I put it in the glass with some water and tried to give it to her but she started to struggle. The glass smashed and she kept shouting. I was terrified that she would wake up the whole street so I… I…' The voice tailed off again.

'Smothered her,' said Blizzard.

Robert nodded and his body was wracked by huge sobs once more.

'With my hand,' he said. He looked at the detectives with desperation in his eyes. 'But I didn't mean to kill her. You have to believe me. She was so frail. I hardly used any force at all…'

'You didn't need to,' said Blizzard. 'Surely, you realised that?'

Emotion overwhelmed Robert again.

'God forgive me,' he mumbled through the tears.

'It's not God you need to worry about,' said Blizzard. 'It's everyone else.'

The inspector left the room and walked down the waiting room near reception. Pausing to compose his thoughts, he took a deep breath and opened the door. There sat Janice. She turned bloodshot eyes on him.

'Did he do it?' she asked fearfully. 'Did he kill Granny?'

'Yes, he did.' Blizzard sat down and took her hand.

'Why?' she cried, her body crumpling. 'Why?'

'Because,' said Blizzard. He was surprised to feel a lump in his throat as he thought of his baby son back at home. Thought of Colley's daughter, of Janice's children playing in the garden. 'Because it turns out that you were right – he is a good uncle, after all.'

Chapter thirty-two

Sarah Allatt stood next to David Colley on the platform at Hafton's central railway station and looked around her with alert eyes that gleamed with anticipation.

'Are we sure they'll be here, Sarge?' she asked.

'The guv'nor reckons so.'

It was shortly before 9am the next morning and they were standing next to a kiosk, surveying the busy platform, which was crowded with Saturday shoppers, harassed parents dragging protesting children, and pensioners on away-days to see grandchildren.

'Good work with The Red Lion,' said Colley after a few moments. 'The governor is really chuffed.'

'I'm glad. I thought I'd blown it with him when I argued about Raymond Buglass.'

Colley gave a slight smile.

'One thing I have learnt about John Blizzard over the years,' he said, 'is that you are OK to argue with him as long as you do it the right way – and as long as you realise that he is always right.'

Allatt gave a low laugh.

'I'll bear it in mind,' she said. She looked along the platform. 'No sign of them. What did the B & B owner say when he called in again?'

'Just that he was suspicious about a couple staying with him last night. Said they looked nervous and that one of them was a Londoner. We suspect that they had been lying low until the fuss dies down. He overheard one of them say that they were going to get out of the city by train this morning.'

Allatt looked up to the other end of the platform, where lounging against a pillar next to the toilet block was Chris Ramsey, dressed in black anorak and jeans and pretending to read a newspaper. Other plainclothes officers were dotted around the station and Blizzard was sitting on one of the benches, apparently reading a magazine although his surreptitious glances belied his real intention. He caught Colley's eye and the sergeant shook his head.

Allatt turned to look along the platform again, stiffening as she did so.

'Bingo,' she said.

Colley followed her gaze and saw Marion Rowbotham and a tall grey-haired man walking from the ticket office towards the platform where the main westbound train was due to arrive in a few moments.

'Good spot,' said Colley.

He looked at Blizzard and gestured in their direction and within seconds, the inspector and Ramsey were walking quickly down the platform whilst Colley and Allatt closed in from the other direction, followed by another couple of plainclothes officers and, behind them, two uniformed transport policeman. As they neared the couple, De Montfort spotted the movement and gave a frantic tug at Marion's sleeve. She turned and cried out.

De Montfort barged past an elderly woman who was seeing off a friend and leapt onto the nearest train, which was about to depart. Marion followed him as did Blizzard and Ramsey, narrowly avoiding being trapped by the sliding door while Colley ordered a startled guard to halt the train. It was John Blizzard who encountered the suspects first, entering the nearest carriage and seeing them edging their way along the aisle as the train started to grind to a halt.

'Don't come any nearer,' snarled De Montfort.

Marion eyed them with alarm then turned at a hissing sound behind her as the doors slid open and Colley and Allatt entered the coach. She started to cry.

'It's all over, Paul,' said Blizzard quietly.

De Montfort spun on his heel, barged Marion out of the way and raced towards the exit. He struck the startled Colley a hefty blow in the stomach, which sent the sergeant staggering backwards. Colley lost his footing and landed heavily on the platform, groaning as the impact knocked the wind out of him. De Montfort lashed out at Allatt, knocking her sideways, and jumped onto the platform where he hurdled the dazed Colley, who was sprawled on the ground fighting for breath.

'Get him!' shouted Blizzard.

Allatt jumped from the carriage and gave chase as De Montfort, defying his age, sprinted down the platform, through the scattering crowds. Starting to breathe heavily, he stopped at the foot of the bridge over the line to the next platform then ran up the stairs, followed by the rapidly closing Allatt. At the top, he stumbled and before he could recover his balance, the constable was on to him. De Montfort roared with rage and snapped out a fist, sending her crashing into the railings, but recovering herself immediately, she dived forward in a rugby tackle as he tried to run away again and the two of them hit the floor hard. Lying half-winded, Paul De Montfort gave a feeble groan as the constable snapped on the handcuffs just as Ramsey and Colley appeared at the end of the bridge, followed by the wheezing Blizzard.

Trying to ignore his spinning head, Colley walked up to where Allatt was dragging the groggy De Montfort to his feet.

'You don't fancy playing for us this afternoon, do you, Sarah?' he said. 'That was the best damned tackle I have ever seen in a long time.'

'Read him his rights, Sarah,' said Blizzard.

'Me?'

'Yeah, this is your collar. I promised you that I wouldn't leave you out, didn't I?'

'You did, guv,' she said cheerfully.

She read De Montfort his rights then started to lead him across the bridge. De Montfort glanced over the parapet down to where a sobbing Marion Rowbotham was being escorted along the platform by two transport policemen.

'I guess that's it then,' he said, looking back at Blizzard.

'Just about,' said the inspector.

He and Colley interviewed De Montfort shortly after eleven that morning in the room at Abbey Road where Eric and Robert Leys had both sat the day before. Dressed in his smart blazer and grey slacks, now muddied from the incident at the platform, De Montfort still cut an urbane figure.

'So, which one of you is The Latch Man?' asked Blizzard. 'Denny, I assume?'

The duty solicitor opened his mouth to say something but Blizzard beat him to it.

'An objection already?' he asked.

'I have only had chance for the briefest of conversations with my client,' said the lawyer. 'And in view of that, I would like to request that we adj–'

'Oh, just let him answer the bloody questions,' said Blizzard wearily. 'Frankly, I'm sick of people holding out on me.'

The lawyer glared at him, Colley's face displayed just the merest hint of a smile and De Montfort hesitated for a moment then gave a shrug. The game was up. He knew it, the lawyer knew it and Blizzard and Colley knew it.

'So, I ask again,' said Blizzard. 'Which one of you was The Latch Man?'

'Denny,' said De Montfort in that cultured voice of his, which Blizzard and Colley had instantly recognised from the night in Garden Street Railway Station. 'The latch thing was his idea. He had style, did Denny.'

'You knew him from the old days, I think?' asked the inspector.

'I used to fence stuff for him but I hadn't seen him for years. When he came out of prison, he said he was not interested any more. I tried to persuade him – we were making a lot of money – but he would not change his mind.'

'But you still kept fencing stuff for other people?'

'Only when something tasty came onto the market. There's always someone prepared to take a chance for a nice piece of antique jewellery. Your lot got close to me a few times in London but they were never able to pin anything on me.'

De Montfort looked round.

'Do you know,' he said, 'I have not been in a police interview room for many years.'

'And Marion Rowbotham?' asked Blizzard, ignoring the comment. 'Where does she fit into the picture?'

'She and I stepped out for a while when we were much younger. She was working down in London at the time, at a primary school. When she found out what I did for a sideline, she introduced me to Denny. They had known each other since they were children, went to school together, and I think he had a thing for her. If he resented us, he never said anything. Too much of a gentleman, was Denny.'

'Was she ever involved in the business? Handling some of the stolen gear?'

'Not really,' said De Montfort. 'She liked the money but the bright lights faded after a while. She only ever really wanted to teach. That's how she ended up going back to Hafton. Got a job up here.'

'You did not follow her?'

'I did not really fancy living in the north.' He gave a slight smile. 'Too many whippets and flat caps for me. But we kept in touch, the odd phone call, Christmas cards, that kind of thing. She came to visit me in London a few times, but it was never like the old times.'

'So how come you hooked up with Denny Buglass again?' asked Blizzard. 'I mean, after all these years?'

'Marion met him at an art night class. At Hafton College. Watercolours, as I recall. Wouldn't have thought it was his thing really, but there you go. Denny told her that his business was in trouble. He'd sold his shop at a loss and his new one wasn't doing very well. He'd tried to get a loan from the banks but they didn't want to know. He'd even tried a moneylender. His son put him in touch with the guy.'

'Not a chap by the name of Jackie Rowlands, by any chance?' asked Blizzard.

'I think that was him. It didn't go well, anyway. The guy charged extortionate rates and got heavy when Denny fell behind on the repayments. Marion suggested that he start thieving again. She rang me and we came to an agreement.'

'He told us that he had been straight for years,' said Colley.

'He had and he didn't want to do it, but he'd have done anything to save his business. And he wanted to get things straightened out so that he could give something to his son. Help him pay off the moneylender. And before you ask, the lad had no idea that his dad was thieving again.' De Montfort shook his head. 'It was remarkable, though. Denny had lost none of his skills.'

'But surely, he realised it was only a matter of time before we came around to him?' said Blizzard.

'He reckoned that all the coppers from the old days would have gone. Besides, like he said, even if anyone did make the connection, who would suspect someone his age with a bad back?'

'So why the scene at Garden Street Railway Station?'

'I didn't know how close you were to us and that press conference really shook me up. I thought that if I could get you looking at someone other than The Latch Man for the murder of Edith Bradley, it might buy us a bit of time. It gave me the chance to get back to London. I planned never to come back but Denny was in pieces about what had happened to the old girl.'

'So, do we take it that he killed her?' asked Colley.

'It was never the plan. It was supposed to be a clean job, like all the others, in and out.'

'Why her?' asked Blizzard.

'Marion heard that she kept a lot of money in the house. Edith disturbed Denny and he panicked.'

'But violence was not his style, surely.'

'Denny knew that prison would kill him and he was worried about what would happen to his son if he wasn't around.'

'I take it that you were the one who murdered him at the guest house?'

De Montfort nodded sadly.

'I didn't want to,' he said, 'but he was going to tell you everything. Said he could not live with what he had done. I couldn't let that happen. I mean, look at me, I take thirteen tablets a day. Do you really think that I will last the distance in prison? None of us are getting any younger, are we?'

'No,' said Blizzard. 'No, we're not.'

* * *

An hour later, the officers were hearing the same story from Marion Rowbotham in the same interview room.

'You had us all fooled, I'll give you that,' said Blizzard.

Marion smiled.

'It's all about leopards,' she said.

'Leopards?'

'They never can change their spots. It's the same with villains. Crime is a drug to them, Chief Inspector, they just keep coming back to it. Denny was a villain, Eric was a villain, my dad was a villain, Paul is a villain. And I suppose, so am I. It's in the blood. It's a simple law really.'

'Yes, it is.' Blizzard sat back in his chair, assailed by a great sensation of weariness. 'But one I forgot.'

'It's all about stakes, Chief Inspector. If they are high enough, a person can do anything.'

Blizzard thought of the cowed figure of Robert Leys sitting in his cell, eyes red raw with crying, façade of studied indifference finally shattered by the enormity of what he had done.

'Yes,' he said softly, 'I think they can.'

Chapter thirty-three

'Well done, John,' said Arthur Ronald as he placed a mug of tea on his desk in front of the inspector much later that afternoon. He gave him an approving nod. 'Well done, indeed. Three murders detected, one that we did not even know had been committed and the mystery of The Latch Man solved. That's remarkable by anyone's standards, I'd say. I take it that they were interesting enough for you?'

Blizzard gave his friend a rueful look.

'Perhaps I should keep my mouth shut in future,' he said.

'It's a good job you didn't. No one would have known that Doris had been murdered if you hadn't stuck to your guns. No, you've excelled yourself.'

'I guess.' Blizzard took a sip of tea. 'But it was all down to the team, of course.'

'You can cut the false modesty with me. It was down to you and we both know it.'

'Thank you.' Embarrassed by the praise, the inspector sought to take a business-like approach. 'Has Chris Ramsey told you that we got the guys who were with Leys and Bradley?'

'No, he hasn't. That's good news.'

'Yeah, Gerry Lawson was arrested trying to get onto the ferry back to Rotterdam and the other guy was picked up at a flat over on the north side of the city. Oh, and Sophie van Beek is coming back from Rotterdam on Wednesday to see how we can make sure that Eric Leys is brought to book for threatening their officers.'

'She'll have to get in the queue.'

'How's that?'

'Well, for a start, the Spanish cops want to talk to him about a couple of unsolved murders – two expat drug dealers shot dead in a Malaga bar ten years ago.'

'Well, me and David have got some holiday time owing. Maybe you could send us on a nice jolly?'

'And maybe not. I hate to sound pernickety but I'm still waiting for you to send me that budget report…'

'You're never satisfied, are you?' said Blizzard but he was smiling. 'You mentioned a queue? Eric Leys in demand, is he?'

'Just a bit,' said Ronald. 'I've had an email from the police in Mexico about some offences that they want to discuss with him. Couple of shootings. Oh, and Jim Corbett's governor rang me to say that the Fraud Squad fancy a crack at money laundering charges as well. God knows how I'm going to keep them all happy.'

'You'll be fine. You're good at the diplomatic stuff.'

'Unfortunately, yes.' A thought struck him. 'What about Martin Hornsby? Have we tracked him down yet?'

'Not yet. Looks like he's abandoned Myra and had it away on his toes – him and all the money.'

'We'll get him one day.'

'Maybe.' Blizzard glanced at the wall clock: 5.10.

'About time,' said Ronald.

'Yup.' Blizzard drained his mug and stood up. 'I owe Jim Corbett a pint if this works. We should have thought of it earlier.'

* * *

Half an hour later, Blizzard met up with Colley, Allatt and Jim Corbett outside The Red Lion public house, which stood in a seedy backstreet on the edge of the city centre. A police minibus pulled up and a number of officers in riot gear alighted.

'OK,' said Blizzard. 'Let's go.'

The officers poured into the pub, shouting their warnings and startling the small number of drinkers. Blizzard walked up to a squab-nosed man sitting at the bar.

'What do you want?' said Jackie Rowlands with a scowl.

'To arrest you.'

'Yeah, well you've tried that before. You'll not get anyone to give evidence against me.'

'Not sure that I need to this time. See, your bank statements have told us everything we need to know. Jackie Rowlands, I am arresting you under–' Blizzard glanced at Corbett. 'I knew I'd forget it. What's the legislation again, Jim?'

'Article 60B of the Financial Services and Markets Act 2000. Illegal moneylending.'

'What he said,' offered Blizzard.

Before Rowlands could react, the inspector had applied the handcuffs and the prisoner was being led out of the pub by a couple of uniformed officers. Two hours later, with Rowlands and several other men locked up in the cells at Abbey Road Police Station, Arthur Ronald walked into the inspector's office where Blizzard was completing his paperwork.

'Now that's what I call a good day's work,' said Ronald. He glanced at the wall clock. 'I've checked with the CPS and you're OK to interview Rowlands and the others in the morning. Time for you to go home and see that little 'un of yours, I think. You've hardly seen him lately.'

'You're right,' said Blizzard. He stood up. 'But I have one last job to do before I go – a question that I really do need answering.'

* * *

Shortly before 9.30pm, Blizzard was sitting on the bed in Bill Gordon's room at the Thorntree Home. Gordon was in his chair, eyes bright as he listened to the chief inspector's tale.

'I always had my suspicions,' said Gordon. 'The road accident never really sounded convincing. And one of your lads shot Tony Bradley, I hear.'

The inspector nodded.

'That's my kind of policing,' said the old man approvingly.

'Talking about your kind of policing, every villain I talk to from those days says that you were bent.'

'Really?' Gordon's returning gaze was calm.

'Fitted people up, invented statements, took backhanders. You and your sergeant. They reckon you were both at it. Is it true, Bill?'

'Like I said, they were different days.' With a knowing smile, he picked up his newspaper. 'Good night to you, Chief Inspector.'

***

It was just after 10.30pm when a weary Blizzard got home to find Fee sitting watching the television.

'Hello, stranger,' she said as he walked into the living room and slumped into the armchair.

'Yeah, sorry about that, love. You know how it is.'

'I do.' She pointed to a bottle sitting on an occasional table. 'There's some red left, if you fancy it. You'll have to get yourself a glass. I don't know if you've eaten, but there's a pizza in the freezer.'

'Sounds good.'

After Blizzard had eaten and filled Fee in on the details of the day, she looked at him.

'I've made a decision,' she said. 'I'm not going back to work.'

'You're not?' He stared at her. 'But you love the job.'

'But so do you and one of us has to be there for Mikey.'

'Well, maybe, I can take more days…'

She shook her head.

'I don't think so, John,' she said. 'Oh, don't look like that, love. Somehow, I can't see you at the village play group with all those mums. Can you? No, it's my decision and I'm happy that I've made it. It's for the best.'

The conversation was interrupted by crying from upstairs.

'I'll go,' said Blizzard, standing up.

Fee smiled affectionately at him.

'You do that,' she said and touched his arm lightly as he walked past her.

THE END

Character list

Hafton police officers:

DCI John Blizzard – head of Western Division CID
DI Graham Ross – head of forensics in Western Division
DI Chris Ramsey
DS David Colley
DC Fee Ellis – Blizzard's girlfriend and mother of his child
DC Sarah Allatt
PC Jane Eeles
PC Eddie Garbutt
DC Gary Romanes
John Ferris – forensics officer
Andy Green – forensics officer

County force:

Detective Superintendent Arthur Ronald – head of CID in the southern half of the force (which includes Western Division)
DS Jim Corbett – fraud squad
Matt Sparkbrook – firearms inspector

The Hornsby family:

Doris Hornsby – matriarch
George Leys – Doris's first husband
Alf Hornsby – Doris's second husband
Eric Leys – Doris's son
Martin Hornsby – Doris's son
Myra Hornsby – Martin's wife
Janice Poulter – Doris's granddaughter
Robert Leys – Doris's grandson

Others:

Edith Bradley – pensioner
Tony Bradley – Edith's son
Dr Richard Brewis – GP
Denny Buglass – corner shop owner
Raymond Buglass – Denny's son
Edgar Cole – lawyer
Jay Colley – David Colley's wife
Bill Gordon – retired detective
Geoff Hays – drug dealer
Paul de Montfort – London antiques dealer
Tommy Fearnley – London criminal
Erroll Hayles – hotel owner
Terry Hibbs – petty criminal
Gerry Lawson – drug dealer
Brian Makepeace – drug dealer
Annie Meadows – nurse
Peter Reynolds – Home Office pathologist
Gareth Robinson – London criminal
Marion Rowbotham – Caitby Mallard resident
Jackie Rowlands – illegal moneylender
Reverend Sparks – vicar of Caitby Mallard
Sophie van Beek – Dutch police officer

If you enjoyed this book, please let others know by leaving a quick review on Amazon. Also, if you spot anything untoward in the paperback, get in touch. We strive for the best quality and appreciate reader feedback.

editor@thebookfolks.com

www.thebookfolks.com

ALSO BY JOHN DEAN

In this series:

The Long Dead (Book 1)
Strange Little Girl (Book 2)
The Railway Man (Book 3)
The Secrets Man (Book 4)
A Breach of Trust (Book 5)
Death List (Book 6)
A Flicker in the Night (Book 7)

In the DCI Jack Harris series:

Dead Hill
The Vixen's Scream
To Die Alone
To Honour the Dead
Thou Shalt Kill
Error of Judgement
The Killing Line

Writing as John Stanley:

The Numbers Game
Sentinel

All available on Kindle and in paperback.

When a routine archaeological dig turns up bodies on the site of a WWII prisoner of war camp, it should be an open and shut case for detective John Blizzard. But forensics discover one of the deaths is more recent and the force have a murder investigation on their hands.

When a family is brutally murdered, one child is never found. It still troubles DCI John Blizzard to this day. But new clues emerge that will take him deep into the criminal underworld and into conflict with the powers that be. Cracking the case will take all of the detective's skills, and more. Coming out unscarred will be impossible.

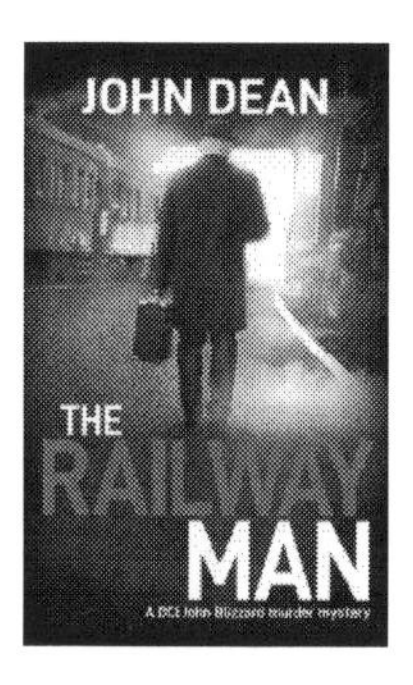

Veteran crime-solver DCI John Blizzard is confronted with his hardest case yet when a boxer and wide boy is found dead in a railway signal box. Someone is determined to ruin the investigation and prepared to draw the residents of a local housing estate into a war with the police to get their way. Has the detective finally met his match?

While detective John Blizzard looks into a series of drug-related deaths, his nemesis, gangland thug Morrie Raynor, is released from prison. Blizzard becomes convinced Raynor is linked to a new crime spree, but with little evidence other than the ravings of a sick, delirious man, the detective's colleagues suspect his personal feelings are clouding his judgement.

A corrupt industrialist is found dead in his home. When his family shed crocodile tears, DCI John Blizzard turns the screw. But when their alibis check out, can his team track down the real killer among a long list of likely suspects?

An undercover detective is shot in his home. Later, police officers on a routine patrol are fired at. Someone has a big problem with law enforcement. DCI Blizzard starts a crackdown on his city's most notorious gangsters. But is he in danger of rubbing the wrong people up the wrong way? Or is he already on the killer's list?

Someone is starting deadly fires, but the only clue to their identity is the obscure poetry that DCI John Blizzard receives on his desk. Taunting the police is one thing. Taunting Blizzard another. He'll stop at nothing to crack the case and collar the arsonist.

Visit www.thebookfolks.com for more great titles like these!